IRON SHINTO

by

Tricia Stewart Shiu

Illustrations and Cover Photo
by Sydney Shiu

IRON SHINTO
by Tricia Stewart Shiu
Illustrations and Cover Photo by Sydney Shiu

Copyright © 2013 by Tricia Stewart Shiu

Published by Human Being Publishing

ISBN: 978-0-9840020-8-5

Licensing Notes

ISBN: 0984002081
ISBN 13:   9780984002085

Acknowledgments

Thank you to: Sydney Shiu, Eric Shiu, Glenn Stewart, Rebecca Gummere, Harry Stewart, Betsy Stewart, Kristin Palombo, Suzan Olson, Dr. Kimbal Ian Moise, Vivienne Williamson, Lin Morel and Suzan Olson Davis, Gloria Ginn and David.

"Battle not with monsters lest you become one."

– Friedrich Nietzsche

Table of Contents

Prologue
The Prince of Jupiter

It has been said that gods ruled as kings before Earth was formed. The people who said this, however, never met the Prince of Jupiter, who single-handedly transported the inhabitants of Jupiter beyond their meager planetary confines to a world where desires were manifested with a thought and dreams were a three-dimensional reality. It was all because of a glorious, mystical accident.

As a boy, the prince was fascinated with the afterlife and spent every waking moment studying what happens at the moment of death. He learned that the physical body contains two distinct ethereal bodies, the "Ba" and "Ka." The "Ba" or soul leaves the body at the moment of death and returns to a collective group of souls where it will reincarnate into another body. The "Ka" departs the body but stays nearby. It remains a psychic imprint or "spirit" which can roam freely but remains detached. It was the "Ka" body that fascinated the prince the most. The "Ka" can make journeys to heaven, hell or can relive its human life for eternity.

The prince wondered what could happen to the "Ka" while the body was still alive. His curiosity led him to a meditation practice in which he attempted to send his own

"Ka" on "errands." He became quite adept at allowing his "Ka" out for short excursions and equally skillful at calling it back into his physical body.

As the prince continued his unorthodox self-guided education, the queen, who had fallen ill shortly after the prince was born, spent most of her time in bed, which left it to the king to raise and care for the prince. Despite the stressful family arrangement, the king dedicated himself to giving the increasingly overcrowded planet of Jupiter some much-needed elbow room. The king's initial exploratory missions found a suitable planet called Earth. Although the atmosphere was not ideal, the royal metaphysicists had created alchemical conveyance structures—pyramids—which would allow any Jupiterian to materialize on any planet and to calibrate to the atmosphere.

The first exploratory excursions to Earth found locations for three conveyance structures. Metaphysicists also calculated that one year on Jupiter equaled one hundred years on Earth. Construction of the pyramid conveyance structures—PCSs—

began when the prince was a baby and concluded when he was fifteen. The aim was to link other PCSs with energetic vortices on the planet Earth and constellations beyond Jupiter's galaxy. Each PCS included two transportation areas: The King's Chamber and the Queen's Chamber.

What no one could have planned, however, was how the PCSs, now located around the world, would react with the intensely powerful, naturally occurring healing vortices on Earth and the prince's "Ka" exercises.

The young prince begged his father for permission to be part of the first test group for the newly erected pyramids. When his father refused, the prince sent his "Ka" body into a PCS where it successfully rematerialized on Earth! Although his "Ka" was separated from his physical body, the prince experienced all sensations on Earth as if he had a physical body. As he exited the main portal into Earth's atmosphere, he accidentally cut his hand on a sharp crystal at the mouth of the pyramid. Wrapping his hand in his cloak, he continued on his adventure. The prince explored the lush foliage surrounding the PCS and the crystal-blue waters, which flowed nearby. He dipped his hand into the lake to test the temperature and his cut healed immediately!

Upon his return and after he had reintegrated his "Ka" into his physical body, the Prince was punished by the king for his disobedience. He promised he would never attempt to travel through a PCS or release his "Ka" again. Meanwhile, the PCS project fell out of fashion. Most Jupiterians, it turned out, would rather not travel through the PCSs but favored their newly developed astro vehicles instead. So the project was abandoned.

By the time the prince was twenty, his fascination with using the portals turned to a full obsession. Based on his own healing experience with the beautiful crystal lake he wondered if a PCS could access the incredible healing powers of Earth for his mother, so he once again begged his father to go back but his father was still mistrustful.

Legend says that the prince convinced his father to allow him to separate each of their "Ka" bodies, including his mother—now, gravely ill—and they would go, as a family, through the portal for healing. When they arrived on Earth, however, they found that all the lakes and foliage had turned to desert. Sadly, when the family tried to return to Jupiter, the PCS failed. They remained suspended on Earth in stasis. Their "Ka" bodies were all they had, and so, with no kingdom to return to, the family set about building an invisible virtual kingdom. Invisible, that is, until they were discovered by the Anuenue. These entities were the bridge to the other world. The Anuenue told them that their PCS had been overtaken by the Egyptians—who could not see or hear the royal family because of their vibrational state—and the PCS was renamed the Great Pyramid. Egyptians believed the pyramid was constructed by pharaohs as a burial tomb. The only chance of rescuing the Royal Jupiterian family from imprisonment was through the power held within a statue created in honor of a young man who died at the base of the pyramid. The Legendary Ku was the only human in Earth history whose "Ka" and "Ba" were transferred directly into the statue where they remained intact. The Anuenue said that they would find the statue and, through Earth inhabitants, find a way to free the royal family from eternal imprisonment.

A group of benevolent Earth women was chosen for this task and was given guidance through Moa, a mystic guide. What the Anuenue did not tell the royal family was that the statue alone could not help them; instead, they would need a special stone to activate the statue and thus heal the queen. Moa placed the stone into the statue to release the royal family from their stasis.

While the royal family was on Earth, they tried several times, in vain, to return home through other PCSs on Earth. Their final attempt at escaping through an Earth vortex in Japan was thwarted by an evil force, which came in the form of a spindly-limbed crone. This evil force was fed on the stolen gifts.

With the Anuenue's help, the king imprisoned the evil crone in a stone temple, which he embedded in the forests of Egypt.

She remained there until a young Ku freed her from her confines after which she fled to the island of Japan. His good deed bound Ku and the crone together for the remainder of Ku's Earth life and eventually caused his demise.

The king felt that the PCS from Japan—called the Iron Shinto—was safer with him than in the hands of such an evil force, so he shrank it and transported it to his virtual palace for safekeeping.

CHAPTER I

Continuum

Ritual: Connecting the Dots
Element: Copper
Planet: Venus

Lie quietly and listen to your breathing. Inhale fully and deeply sixty times. Imagine a light in your heart space, which grows beyond your body and surrounds you with protective light.

Now, imagine a line of relatives from your past extending behind you. Even if you don't know who they are, see them stretching in a timeline back as far as you can visualize. In front of you, imagine a line of relatives forming. Again, you don't have to understand what you see or if you know these people. Then, feel your heart space light extending backward and forward in time to each of the relatives in your lineage. See that lovely healing heart light mending any past troubles or patterns. Then imagine that the light is moving through you and beyond you, extending into the future, healing all that was, is and will be.

Hillary writhes in pain on a crinkly paper-covered table. Acupuncture needles protrude from her hands, her stomach and her face. Her eyes are wide with fear as she quickly glances down at her wrists and ankles, which are bound by thick, oiled leather restraints. Her hands look different, small child-like hands, slim short fingers with bitten nails. Her tiny feet have even tinier toes. The sound of city traffic wafts in through the rusty security bars of a dirty window as her gaze wanders to an ornate tattoo curling around her right ankle.

The reality almost chokes the breath from her pincushion chest. She is inhabiting someone else's body. And who on earth, she wonders, would tattoo a child?

"If you just close your eyes, you will gain so much more from this process, miss." The doctor jabs a needle directly into her forehead and turns it again and again.

Hillary tries to jerk away, but her restraints prohibit almost all movement. Pain jaggedly zings through her head. It certainly feels like it's Hillary's body, or at least this pain is happening to her.

"Mommy?" Shocked at the rasp of her voice and that she is calling out for her mother—an act she hasn't done since she was ten, more than eight years ago—Hillary cranes her neck to find any evidence of her location.

The doctor wears thick black-framed glasses with even thicker lenses and he reaches over Hillary to turn the needle in her left forearm. As he does so, his grimy, stained sleeve brushes across her lips and she wonders how often he launders his lab coats. His manner is cool and cruel and as she winces, he gives a slight smile. "How is it said? No pain, no gain?"

His worn black work shoes squeak on the beige tiled floor as he leaves. Hillary feels the wake of cool air pass over her body, hears the creak of the door handle and, finally, the metallic clunk as the doctor slides the deadbolt into place.

Resisting the urge to close her eyes, Hillary can't explain it, but there is something she does not wish to see which lurks just behind her eyelids. She blinks. The blink turns into a flutter and before she knows it, her eyes shut.

The second her upper lashes meet her lower lid, she gasps. Her own face appears inches from her nose. It's as if she has separated from her body and a part of her is unreasonably close.

Eyes snapping open, brakes squeal on the street below followed by a loud crash, then people arguing in an indiscernible foreign language. Hillary frantically scans the immediate area for anyone, her breath comes in heaves, as if whoever, whatever, was hovering above her was pressing on her chest. No one is in the room. Outside, a gentle rain drips through an ancient barred window and falls onto a rolling metal cart containing cotton balls, a large bottle of alcohol and the dreaded needles.

Struggling to free herself, she yanks at one arm restraint, then another. A wisp of a thought meanders through her mind. Is it really worth all the trouble being here on Earth? The thick leather burns her wrists, almost rubbed raw, as she writhes against them, willing them to give under her pressure. Feeling no release, Hillary examines the bound right wrist of her prison-body. Perhaps it will hold a clue to whoever is encasing her ethereal body and maybe the evidence will offer information about how she can escape. Again, slightly stronger, the meandering thought continues.

Wouldn't it be easier to be set free of the confines of this human body? The right wrist has thick, horizontal pink scars just at the inside crease. Oh God, Hillary jolts in disbelief. This child tried to commit suicide. A quick glance confirms her worst fears, the same scarring on the left one. Both hands have scratches and the nails are dirty and bitten to the nub. Hillary is overcome with pity and, instead of feeling trapped, now wonders if she could be an unwelcome squatter. As she lowers the left hand, it knocks against a small, hard object. Deftly maneuvering her hand into the ample folds of her well-worn fabric of the skirt, she digs into a deep, loose pocket and unearths a small silver coin with a shockingly familiar pattern, three parallel wavy lines.

Suddenly, Hillary hears the acupuncturist's voice and quickly shoves the coin back in the pocket. Before she can do anything else, a snowy white overtakes her vision and a tunnel-like echo engulfs her ears. The veil thins and then fades to nothingness.

"Mommy?" Seven-year-old Heidi's voice is clear and crisp.

Hillary shakes off her jarring experience and hears her sister Molly answering her daughter, the sound vibrating around her head, "Yyyesss."

"Mol, Heidi. Are you okay? Is baby Adem with you?" Hillary's voice sounds thick and she feels numb and warm as she moves her hand to her own light brown curly hair. Wondering if the other thing was a dream, she traces a path to her eyes, her smallish nose and her full lips.

Even though she can't see her niece and sister, she tries to picture each of them as they speak. In her mind's eye, she sees Heidi with her long, straight, light-brown hair, sparking dark brown eyes and bright skirt and top. She imagines Molly's jaw is set sternly—even in relaxation—her own gorgeous wavy light brown bob curling slightly at her chin and her compassionate amber eyes staring directly into Hillary's heart.

Being in this place that is no place is definitely an unusual sensation, like when any of Hillary's limbs fall asleep they feel tingly and cool and just a little uncomfortable, although this is all over her body. And she is definitely awake. In fact, her entire body feels vibrant and alive.

"Sure, Hil." Molly's scared, Hillary can tell. Her trademark skepticism is replaced by taut fear. "Your voice sounds strange. Almost like you're miles away and at the same time right next to me."

"I wonder if Moa is close by. It sure would be nice to have some guidance." Molly pulls Heidi a little closer and yells, "Hello! Moa? Are you there?"

She is met with a tingling silence. Molly's words resonate around the group and echo like a vast cavern.

Heidi senses her mother's tension. "I think Moa is in a different place right now," she says, reaching for her mother's hand. "I feel funny." Heidi rubs her free hand on the entwined hands, tracing each finger as a reassurance that she and her mother are still connected. The idea that no one can see her sends a chill through her little body.

The air smells electric, almost like after a rainstorm, clean and bright.

In this space, Hillary notices that while her sister Molly's voice sounds tinny, her niece Heidi's words ring like a bell. Hillary experiments with her own sound and says, "I hope we come out of this soon. I feel strange—unbalanced—like one half of me is here and another is somewhere else." The timbre in her voice sounds like she has her hands over her ears.

"Me too." Molly's voice hums. The vibration reverberates through Hillary making her feel even more uneven. Nonetheless, Molly continues to call for the absent friend/ spirit guide. "Moa? Moa. Mooooaaaaaaa!"

"Mol, this isn't a restaurant where we can call for service." Hillary loves her sister, but sometimes she can be so annoying. Funny, though, feelings seem to be muffled and fleeting in this new space. "Seems like we're on our own... at least for the time being. I'm guessing Moa and Ku have reunited with their families. But that's a good idea about finding guidance." Hillary attempts to yell, but her voice sounds like a chorus of tinkling bells, "Hello! Anyone! Is anyone out there? We need help!"

Nothing. No response.

"Wow. We really are all alone." Molly shivers like a snare drum.

An unfathomable silence overtakes Hillary. Then a terrible thought: What if none of us is alive?

"Mol, Heidi?" Hillary tries to quell her rising panic. She wishes she could see her sister and niece. "Where are you?" She fumbles around desperately trying to find them. Each word Hillary speaks resonates through her, around her and inside her. It's as if she is sitting inside a steel drum and each word is a note.

"We're here, Hil." Suddenly, her sister's voice sounds as if it is right next to her and Hillary jumps.

Stretching her hand outward toward the sound, Hillary feels around for Molly and Heidi. "Where?"

"We're where we were when we all put our hands on the Iron Shinto and left Egypt. Right across from you." Molly says, "I'm holding Heidi on one side and Adem's carrier on the other."

Hillary continues to grope around her immediate area. She cannot feel anything but the rough weathered roof of the Iron Shinto. Her feet don't even feel like they are touching the ground.

"Are we in Japan yet?" Heidi asks. Hillary smiles as she hears her niece's sweet voice.

"That's a good question." Hillary finally touches something and exclaims, "Aha! It's…let's see, I think it's Adem's carrier." Her hand runs over the plastic handle and down to the baby and the soft plump flesh of his leg. "Yes. It's definitely him."

"Where are *we*?" Molly sighs. "I guess that's the real question."

Hillary pats her way across the carrier until she finds Molly's hand and covers it with her own. "My guess is we are hovering somewhere over Tokyo."

"How do you know that?" Molly's hand tightens under Hillary's.

"Because we would have arrived by now, but I can see the lights in my mind's eye. It looks like we are…hovering far above the city." Hillary is as baffled as they are. Her intuitive sense of the situation is that when the group left Egypt, their atoms split and shifted, molecules shuffled and these elements rearranged perfectly to send Hillary, Heidi, Molly and Adem into the ether. "I have a feeling that awful crone who stole Ku's gifts is behind this."

"What if the crone is here?" Heidi's tinkling voice has a hint of shrillness. "And she's keeping us separated from our bodies."

"Look, at least we have each other." Molly feels the buzz of white noise around her. "For now, we can hold hands until we can come up with a way to get out of here."

"You know," Hillary says, her seriousness sounds dull and heavy, like putting a hand on a beating drum. The sound stops at each syllable. "Our bod-ies are still some-where and…" her syncopated speech stops abruptly with no clear ending.

"I think I took a detour before arriving, um, wherever we are…" Hillary stops short unable to continue. Suddenly pictures of little hands and feet with acupuncture needles flash, lightening fast through Hillary's brain and she whispers, "Whoa! Someone's in danger."

"What? Is it us?" Molly's voice sounds like the highest note plucked on a violin.

"Well, yes and no. I saw pictures…"

"I hear her crying." Heidi's tone is heartbreakingly melodic. "She's asking for her mommy."

"Yes, I understand. The girl is trapped." Hillary soothes, "Who is she?"

"We can save her entire family and their descendants!" Heidi says excitedly.

"Now, how are we going to do that given our…um current location, or lack thereof?" Molly reaches for her daughter's hand and pulls her closer.

Hillary tries to intuit their location to no avail. It seems that they are surrounded by an energy that is determined to keep them stuck. Not wanting to scare Heidi, she merely says, "I don't know, but we better do it soon. I think we are in danger, too, if we don't find her."

"What makes you think so?" Heidi asked reluctantly.

"Just a sense." Hillary doesn't want to tell anyone about her out of body acupuncture experience until she is sure if they need to save the girl from a monstrous abuser or from the girl herself.

The Iron Shinto, a weathered and miniaturized version of a real-life Japanese shrine, has dissolved Hillary, Heidi, Molly and Baby Adem into a metaphysical gray area and I am holding them here for my own purposes. But more about me momentarily.

After reading the "Prince of Jupiter" story from the ancient book from the King and Queen's library, the group held the gem gifts from Ku and began to direct their thoughts and intentions on traveling to the island of Japan to retrieve their physical bodies. Each gem was intended to enhance each recipient's personal gift as well as create an entirely new powerful "group gift" if each participant aimed her focus on a desired goal. As they held hands, closed their eyes and focused on traveling to the Island of Japan, everyone, including Baby Adem and the Iron Shinto dissolved into nothingness.

For now, however, they remain between the light and dark. They aren't dead, they aren't alive, time does not exist and they are behind the veil which separates them from all that exists in the physical world.

"When we left the Royal Palace," Hillary says, "our Kas were instantly separated from our bodies. Remember how the tourists couldn't see us as we wandered near the base of the Pyramid?"

"And we could see each other. But wait," Heidi chimes in, "it could have happened before that. Remember when Ku ascended with Moa in his labyrinth? We were blasted with some kind of energy, then, too. What ever happened to the King, Queen and Prince of Jupiter? Did we really have that experience?"

"The whole thing is beyond logic," says Molly, the self-proclaimed "realist" of the group. "But I know what I saw and felt." She is still trying to wrap her head around how they left Egypt and the manner in which their spirits were separated from their physical bodies. Molly imagines how her own newly acquired gift of claircognizance will be enhanced. Her knowing has already helped them locate Ku. With Heidi's gift of clairaudience and Hillary's clairvoyance they should be able to solve any problems that come their way.

What Molly doesn't know is that she, her daughter, Heidi and sister, Hillary, all agreed to help me during this lifetime to procure that which is rightfully mine—a piece of my soul which will bring completion to my work on Earth.

Just as Moa described as she watched Hillary before their fateful meeting, I hover just beyond the "outer shell." However, I am in a self-imposed exile far from Hillary, Heidi and Molly. Light years away, in fact. The period of time has yet to be determined, but the ultimate decision for the end of my spiritual incarceration will cease when I am complete. And by complete, I mean every fragment of me has been returned to its rightful dwelling place inside me, and I am finally able to go home.

In my current incarnation I'm called Mina, and my story is both long and complicated, so perhaps I should start at the beginning. Human lives have a beginning, middle and end to them, just as stories, do. All of these journeys occur in a container called time.

We all have tasks to complete in life. Either we do them and move on to the next journey, or we don't and must repeat the lesson until the task is completed.

Along with the accomplishing of a task comes an element of timing. The timing is a vibration, which connects us to other people and to the earth. By connecting with timing we agree to join a universal chain of events. Those events determine our future.

We also have free will to choose our destiny. With that choice, we can move in infinite directions based on past choices and events. Timing creates a current in which we travel to specific destinations in order to accomplish certain goals. When we complete the tasks and reach a specific goal, a new timing path/channel opens up for us and we move further along that current toward accomplishing the next goal. Whether we know it or not, we all set goals—consciously or unconsciously—and those goals determine the course of our lives. The expectation of outcome is what makes a difference in how difficult or easy, fast or slow, shallow or deep the journey is. In other words, by expecting an outcome we shape the type of journey we can have in a particular journey.

Journeys also have a beginning, middle and an end. When we've accomplished a goal or task, there is a celebration, which ends a journey. Then, we are at a timing crossroads and we have the ability to choose our next journey. Our expectations, thoughts and feelings can shape our journey or even determine it. That person can release expectations (making the journey open up wider to more possibilities, thus making the journey faster) or create specific judgments and expectations (narrowing the journey's path and perhaps slowing down the process.) The journey is fraught with unknown people and circumstances and, at each moment, we are able to choose (by our reaction, thoughts and actions) how to deal with the situation. By doing so, we create timing.

As I said before, each person's journey has a beginning, middle and end and within that journey can be hundreds, thousands or even millions of journeys all with their own structure and timing. Therefore, my story will start at the beginning of my lifelong journey to find wholeness. What I never imagined was that no amount of searching would manifest the help that I needed. It was all a matter of time.

"Doctor can you help my daughter?" My mother's farm-weathered hands desperately convulse with fear as she pushes me toward the imposing male figure. "I cannot handle her..." Eyes dart right and left, "demon's eyes, she has..." She wrings her hands, "We named her for our heroic ancestors, Minamoto Yoritomo..." and paces toward a window with metal bars. "I caught her talking to no one, thin air, she said it is her grandmother."

He peers over his thick dark framed glasses which magnify his eyes far beyond their normal size, hands in pockets jingling coins, as he leans in closer for a look.

My mother continues, "Her grandmother is dead. She writes strange recipes and once performed a ritual to try to bring the chicken I was cooking for dinner back to life. People talk, doctor. Our family will be sent away if this gets out. Mina has brought us much misery. We cannot survive on our own away from the village."

I wish I could look down at my feet, but the doctor's nose is inches from mine as he bathes me in garlic scent. "Demonic possession. Bad for Ainu family. I fix."

Bad for family. Bad for family. The words echo in my head. My ten-year-old brain trying desperately to make sense of why I need to be fixed. Trying so hard to not see what is right in front of me. But, spirits are everywhere and ignoring what was right in front of me had become increasingly difficult. Especially when the spirits asked me to do things for them. It wasn't my fault that these spirits had unfinished business. I cursed this extra sight I had that no one else seemed to possess. My family has had it hard enough as it is. Being an indigenous Japanese, Ainu, we have been ostracized for thousands of years and finally were made to "assimilate." Both my mother and father were Ainu and it was greatly frowned upon when they married and had children. Everyone around us, including their families, wanted them to find suitable mates who would allow the Ainu blood to disperse. The last thing they need is one of their children bringing disgrace on the family. Maybe I am crazy? Perhaps the doctor can help me after all. But there is something strange about him. I can't put my finger on it, but something isn't quite right.

Reaching into the depths of my skirt pocket, I clutch the only thing I have left of my family, a silver coin that was passed down to me from my grandmother. My thumb moves over the three raised parallel lines and the cool metal as I beg my ancestors to protect me from this malevolent man and to free me of this cursed gift.

He escorts my mother out of the room and says once more for emphasis, "I fix."

This glimpse of her as she leaves is, I fear, the last time I will ever see my mother.

CHAPTER II

Ka

Ritual: Mending the Ka
Element: Tin
Planet: Jupiter

Run a warm bath and place one cup of sea salt and one cup of Epsom salt within. A footbath can be used if no bathtub is available. Before entering the bath stand with hands over the water—palms facing down—and say the following:
Bring healing to my body through my soul. Bring calm to my mind through my thoughts. Bring joy to my heart through my connection to Source.
Now step into the bath (or put your feet in the footbath) and get comfortable. Imagine a healing white light emanating from your soul outward. See the light penetrating every cell of your body and releasing anything negative or dark into the salt water. The salt water will draw out, then neutralize any negativity or darkness so when you step out, you will be clear of anything which has been blocking your path.

Rinse off in the shower (or rinse your feet with clear water). Watch the clean water wash the last bits of struggle or worry down the drain; surround yourself with healing white light.
Your energetic body is now whole.

Hillary, Heidi and Molly all share a common thought. Where are their bodies? And what is happening to or rather in their bodies with their essences or "Ka" absent?

The recurring thought reverberates through Hillary's mind: What if they are already dead? Their bodies could be long buried. She imagines her physical body encased in a dark coffin buried deep within the earth. Then her voice begins to break up like a distorted cell phone call. "Oh, guys, I don't feel right, something's off…"

Without warning, Hillary's head begins to throb. Her senses detect that she is in a dark, moist prison. The air she breathes is stifling and hot and she dare not move for fear of….what? It's strange, but she feels as if she will be retaliated against if she breaks free from this horrific sauna-like dungeon. A deafening hissing noise permeates through the dankness. The quick onset of emotion and sensation is overwhelming and Hillary struggles to breathe.

Her arms feel pinned down. Perhaps she's been tied up and someone or something is going to kill her. Her thoughts jump to her sister and niece and she silently prays for their safety as she tries to free herself. The sound of a deathly rattle looms in the distance. Sweat drips down her nose as the frightening noise draws near. She finally frees her left elbow. Panic ensues as she finds her other limbs immobilized, probably the crone's doing. After all, she did mention the evil woman just before she was transported to this hellish place.

Suddenly, Hillary's elbow is whacked by an invisible metal object propelling her hand down, leaving the entire arm completely numb. She screams out in terror, "Aaaaaaaaaaahhhhh."

T he acupuncturist returns to the treatment room and motions to a padded table covered in white paper. "Sit."

My feet remained stuck to the spot on the tiled floor. Frightening images race through my mind's eye—in fact, the spot between my brows is pulsing and feels achy— but I cannot comprehend or decipher these unusual feelings.

He heaves a strong sigh, shakes his head and strides to me, taking my arms in his hands and guiding me backward to a step stool. Then, I willingly take the two steps up to the table and lie down.

"You have troubles." One hand presses my wrist into a thick leather restraint while his other hand buckles the strap into the heavy metal clip. "Your curse of sight brings big problems to your family." He fastens my other wrist and does the same with the restraints around my ankles. "I will fix."

In truth, I am desperate to be fixed. My entire life has been spent bearing the heavy load that my unusual experiences have brought to my family and I. Girls in my village were meant to cook and clean, not foretell untimely deaths or unearth buried family secrets.

But I am not like the other girls in the village. My mind slips back in time, away from the bright lights of this treatment room, back to a time when judgments hadn't marred my heart.

I am six years old. The early morning sun cuts through the trees and lays across my arms as I make my bed. But a dark voice startles me.

"Mina, I am Minamoto Yoritomo, your previous incarnation." He appears as a filmy muscular man with full battle armor and takes up most of my bedroom doorway.

Trying my best to remain calm—this is not my first encounter with an otherworldly spirit—I steady myself by bracing my knee against my mattress. "My parents told me about you. You were the first shogun of Kamakura and you saved Japan. My father showed me pictures of you just last night and said he and mother named me after you because you were a brave warrior known for your discernment and cleverness in battle."

"You are a worthy namesake, for you are clever as well. I come to you now, to tell you it is imperative that you help yourself and our entire lineage. Our agreement as we travel on earth is to right the wrongs which occurred in previous lifetimes. Some call this righting of wrongs, "karma." In order to stop the karma carried from one lifetime to another, you must travel to the Iron Shinto and retrieve our inner voice," the spirit said.

"I did not agree to anything." I take a cautious step away from the strange messenger.

"You agreed before you were born," he says gently. "The human birth process erases most of our memories between lives, many agreements are forgotten and usually play out over a lifetime. But, you must remember, Mina."

The spirit flashes a series of pictures in my mind which become more and more familiar. First, he shows me pictures of my training as a young boy during his lifetime, receiving my own katana—a battle sword—then, I see myself training late into the night learning special methods, such as the Sage Variation and the Kasugai Dome. Finally, the spirit shows me a battle scene in which I am injured but survive.

More convinced, but still wary, I ask, "Why do I need to travel such a long distance to retrieve it. If you're a spirit, why not get it yourself?"

"You are a clever girl, Mina. I made a grave error during my lifetime. I agreed to relinquish my conscience for Japan to remain safe for eternity. Earth is bound by its own rules of space and time. Within the context of these rules are forces, which enable life to be sustained. Beyond, good and evil, light and darkness, the forces rule existence and non-existence. The closer to Source energy one gets, the more fully one exists however, there is a polarity, which pulls towards non-existence as well. Good and light are in varying degrees closer to a higher level of existence and evil and darkness are closer to the lower level of non-existence."

He takes a moment to allow the information to sink in, then continues. "Well into my rule as Shogun, I received a message from another clan which said that some of the warriors under my tutelage had contacted them about planning a coup. The message named my most honored friend as the leader. The message said further that the rival clan held five of these men in their palace prison and were waiting for me to vouch for their innocence. I felt so betrayed by these men but decided to sleep on my decision so I might see it with fresh eyes in the morning. During the night, I had a dream that a man, who called himself the King of Jupiter, pleaded with me to speak up for these men. In the dream, I argued that I'd had my suspicions about my warriors and perhaps they deserved their punishment. The King explained that this was about so much more than the lives at stake, this was a soul test and if I did not speak the truth, "my truth" is what he said, not only would these men die, but my inner voice would be imprisoned until another family member could pass the test. I told him I could not relinquish my honor and I closed my mind to him. As I did so, a beam of light entered my dreams, encased my inner voice and disappeared. I sent no reply to the rival clan and received word from my spies that these men were all hanged and my Shogun rule continued as usual. Mina, it is a piece of yourself that you are retrieving. Because of my actions, you have been forced to bear the burden of my inability to speak. When your soul was born, your inner voice never came with you. Without it, you will have no defense against those who favor the non-existence. I gave up a piece of myself, Mina. If you do not retrieve this item, you are destined to do the same."

"Well, I just won't do it." I resolutely stamp my foot.

"You say that now, however, the path to non-existence is a tricky one, in the blink of an eye, you can agree to things you never thought you would. Or…"

"Or give up a part of yourself without meaning to." I finish his sentence and then nod solemnly. "I promise to help us retrieve that which is ours. No matter what the cost."

"Be careful, Mina."

"Wait!" I say quickly, "How will I identify the inner voice?"

"You'll know it when you see it." Then the spirit of Mina-moto is gone.

Even though, I am only six and the Iron Shinto is far from our rural family home, a sense of finality settles into my bones as I look at my neat and tidy bed. Suddenly, I feel compelled to walk out my room, through our smooth bamboo front door, down our kaseki fossilized stone walkway. My father and I said a prayer as we laid those stones in a row. Each one valued for their contribution here on earth, first as living beings and now as beautiful petrified stones leading "the way to the gods." My father told me this was the indigenous definition of Shinto religion. Smiling, I feel surrounded by protection because, just as father says, "god is everywhere." I make my way past a stack of rocks, our own Shinto shrine, and to the road abutting our house, where I wait until a passing farmer might allow me to take a ride in his cart.

My wish for transport is granted when a farmer wearing frayed green pants driving a sturdy, wooden cart pulls by oxen invites me to ride with him. He wears a wide straw hat made from woven rice reeds and a dark top, which is so worn it was almost see-through. I settle into the back of his cart atop a pile of soft rice reeds and doze on and off during the trip. In between napping I study his unusual hat. The pattern is woven in a very complicated design and I marvel at the delicate detail. On the back is a dried sea star, and tiny shells line the wide brim. The rocky, winding road, which leads first toward the seashore, veers sharply inland and is lined with splendid rows of regal pine trees. Without a word, the kind farmer lets me off at the base of a long wide flight of stone steps extending up to Tsuru-ga-oka hill and the Temple of Hachiman, dedicated to the God of War. Quickly remembering the farmer's kindness, I turn to thank him, only to find he is gone. I look in all directions but there is no sign of him or his cart.

Shrugging off this odd occurrence, I focus my attention up the stone stairs in hopes of locating the Iron Shinto. Three torii or Japanese gates lead the way to the glorious Temple of Hachiman. In my mind's eye, however, I see three robed figures with raised swords and warrior masks, which frighten me and I almost turn back. But, as the leaves of the icho tree rustle behind me, I turn back toward the steps and notice behind the hill two smaller shrines, about half the size of the Temple of Hachiman and made of stacked stone,. No frightening guards stand watch as I creep forward, careful not to disturb my ancient ancestor. The first shrine I encounter is dedicated to the Emperor Nintoku, son of the God of War, who is been called Wakamiya.

Farther down the path stands an unusual structure of ebony and gold with four iron pillars in front. I have arrived at the Shirahata Jinja, which honors Minamoto Yorimoto. The gorgeous, massive tomb is made of limestone, which shimmers in the noonday sun, and the petals of the flowering trees drift over the ground in the gentle summer breeze. I gather some beautiful petals and lay them at the base of the stone altar just inside the door. That's when I notice the wooden carving of Yorimoto. It is a striking image of him—his strong chin, broad shoulders and large muscles are impressive. I kneel before him and say my prayer:

"Please help me find your... I mean *our* inner voice. I don't even know where to begin looking." Pleading with the Yorimoto carving, I gaze deep into the pinhole irises carved into the ancient wood of his eyes. "I came all this way for something you gave away. The least you can do is give me a little guidance." I again scan the wooden face for any trace of reaction. Surely, if he sent me here, he would show himself to me now. Sadly, his small, carved nose and thick lips remained stoic and his eyes stay fixed in a steely stare.

I dust off my simple cotton skirt and rise to leave. But, just as I turn a light behind the Yorimoto image catches my eye. Putting my face up to the crack between stones, I see the most amazing sight! An ornate shrine made entirely of iron stood directly behind the Shirahata Jinja. The Iron Shinto! Quickly, I skip around the structure and gasp at what I encounter upon seeing the entrance.

Although weathered, the incredible details are still intact. I run my hand over intricately designed images all made from metal and feel a buzz through my hand as I do so. The buzzing sensation travels from my hand through my arm as I see a dragon rearing its head at a warrior with a samurai sword. A lovely grove of trees lines a scene with three characters. These people wear clothing I've never seen before and the image includes a strange triangular building as a backdrop.

Suddenly, in the floor right in front of me a whirling blue pool opens up, the crown atop the Queen's head begins to move, the kings flowing robe becomes a rippling purple and the Prince's fingers wiggle. The entire family comes alive and steps out of the carving!

"I am the King of Jupiter, this is my wife the Queen, and here is our son, the Prince."

Without a word, the woman picks me up and presses her cheek close to mine. The King places a strong hand on his son's arm and then strokes my hair. The son's face radiates strength and contentment.

It feels so warm to be in their presence. Never in my life have I felt such comfort and caring. I sense that I could potentially fulfill a deep need that the Queen has—she desperately wants another child. Then in a soft whisper, she says, "You don't have to stay here. Come back with us to Jupiter. You will be loved and nurtured and cared for in a way that cannot be done during your life-time on Earth."

Panic fills my chest. I fear that I might fall short of this incredible family's expectations. Once they find out about my secret of seeing the unseeable, they'll change their mind. I long to follow her, to go to Jupiter, but I remember my life and family. Even if it would benefit me, the obligations I have to my own family far outweigh the desires of the Queen. Oh, but wouldn't it be wonderful to have a mother who truly wants me, a father of notable stature and a kind brother to protect me from the mean boy.

Before I can respond, a shimmering ball of light zips through the threshold and expands into a life-sized column of light. Out steps an old crone from a doorway in the light pillar and says, "Look at me, Mina." Emaciated, her skin hangs off of her bones and her very essence seems deprived, unloved and abandoned. I shudder as she continues, "I suffered for thousands of years because of that man!" She wields her bony, crooked finger as if it is a sword, slashing and jabbing at the King. In retaliation, the King creates a frightening tornado within the Iron Shinto in which I am the center. A chilling stillness permeates my body while inches away, the air, and anything in its path, including the crone, is sucked into its powerful vortex, the wild wind screeching with each rotation.

"Will you come with us?" The King's voice booms over the gale. "If you do not, you will indeed, become her. If that happens we will meet under much different circumstances. Mina, you must choose now!"

Terrified beyond belief, I cover my ears with my hands and begin to cry. To choose between my current life and an unknown one is too much for me to bear.

Then I see it. An iron ball, embedded in metal work. It doesn't exactly match the rest of the artistic style of the ironwork, but is welded in place. I am certain that the iron ball contains the inner voice of my lineage!

Because of the fierce wind whirling around me, I cannot move. The crone stops her screeching and calls to me, "I am you, Mina. This is what you will look like if you choose to follow this man's instructions! Beware!"

How can this woman be me? Is this the type of trickery Minamoto warned me about? The King, Queen and Royal son all gaze at me with pleading eyes. Their images flicker and begin to fade. I can see they are desperate to express the importance of my traveling with them, but no words can reach me. Communication with them is fading.

"Please, may I have that iron ball?" I point to the embedded orb, which I believe contains the lost inner voice of my lineage.

Before they can answer, the crone lets out a screech and with all of her might pushes her hands away from her body in a motion that blasts the Royal group with an explosive force. Their images flicker and I cover my ears as they cry out in desperation, and in one last gesture to get me to choose the King swings his arm in an upward arc, shrinking the Iron Shinto and dissolving it right along with them. Within seconds, I am sitting alone on the grass. The Iron Shinto is gone and there is no trace of its existence. The grass flutters in the now chilly breeze, the sun has gone behind the hill and I attempt to wrap my brain around what has just occurred. Venturing out into the garden near the bottom of those fearsome stone steps, I make my way to the base of the gargantuan icho tree. Three of my family's huts could fit into the tree's trunk. Placing my hands on the smooth bark, I try to imagine what it would be like to be over a thousand years old. I am sure, in its time, that the tree has borne witness to heartache and joy beyond measure. Imagining weddings and funerals, honorific ceremonies and devastating wars, I feel so insignificant that I put my arms out wide and embrace the tree's massive trunk to connect with its wondrous life.

That's when I feel a hand on my back and turn to see a tall keikan, or police officer. He escorts me to his patrol car and, although I ask if he would sound his siren, he says he thinks it would be better if he doesn't. After telling him where I live, he questions how such a little girl could travel so far away. As he smooths his dark mustache, I tell the story of the kind farmer who transported me with his cart. The keikan takes his hand away from his face, places it on the wheel of his patrol car and stares at the setting sun and shakes his head. Farmers stopped using carts to transport their wares about seventy years ago, he tells me, and the one I described sounds much like the legendary farmer, Toromata. The keikan continues to stare flatly at the afterglow on the horizon as he continues his story.

Toromata was known for his charity even though he was extremely poor. He would walk miles to help a neighbor fix a broken plow, mend a fence or heal a sick ox. He was known for wearing a hat with a lone sea star on it and tiny shells, which jingled as he walked.

I nod and agree that this must be the man I encountered on my trip to the shrine.

The keikan sets his jaw firmly and shakes his head. "That is impossible, little one," his eyes turn slowly toward me, and when our gaze meets, he says, "Toromata has been dead for over two hundred years."

We ride in silence for the rest of the trip back to my home.

The keikan looks at my mother's flared nostrils and clenched fists and, finally, at my trembling body. I can feel his ambivalence at delivering me back to an obviously hostile environment. A wave of regret washes over me as I wish back the story I've just shared with this seemingly benevolent man. Why do I always turn perfectly normal situations into uncomfortable ones?

And why had I relinquished the inner voice? I was mere steps away from it while in the Iron Shinto and yet, I failed.

Self-blame weighs heavily in the pit of my stomach when I catch a glimpse of my mother. Her emotionless eyes belie the abject fury contained in her clenched fists. A single tear escapes down my cheek as a group of villagers gather to see the uniformed keikan carefully help me out of his car and gently point me toward my home. I can already see my brothers and sisters and hear the mocking voices.

"Lookie at the kookie!" The village mean boy screeches from his perch on a cherry blossom tree in our neighbors yard. "Mina's craaaaazy. That one is crazzzzzy!" He taunts.

I look back just in time to watch the keikan turning away from me, straightening up and walking to his car.

The acupuncturist stands over me. Bright lights overhead in the treatment room temporarily blind me and the zing of the first needle brings me back from my memory. He pokes the needle into my forearm and then turns it again and again and again. I do my best to breathe through the pain. Perhaps this is the price I must pay to be normal.

Or maybe this is the treatment I deserve.

CHAPTER III

Stuck Scream

Ritual: Clear Sight
Element: Zinc
Planet: Uranus

Sit in a relaxing space where you will remain undisturbed for at least an hour. Rub your hands together quickly until you feel heat in your palms. Then close your eyes and place your palms over your eyes with your fingers resting comfortably on your forehead. Imagine healing energy runs from your palms into your eye sockets relaxing the muscles around your eyeball, in the back of your eye, throughout your entire eye area. Repeat the following incantation as you relax:
I am willing to see my own Light. I am willing to see the Light in all people. I release any blocks to my seeing my own Light. I release any blocks to seeing the Light in all people.

Allow the healing from your hands to sink into your eyes. Imagine that all tension melts into the earth and flows back to Source. You may stay here as long as you'd like.

Your Light will help you see. Know that you are a part of the light and that your Light is a beacon to seeing what you've created.

Hillary tries to scream but the sound is trapped inside her, multiplying the terror she feels.

Her arms and legs have been pinned against a dark immovable force. Suddenly, a picture flashes in her mind—no doubt her newly discovered clairvoyance is bearing a frightening gift—a shocking scene slowly unfolds in her mind's eye. It's as if she is experiencing the emotions in present time.

She sees the crone through Ku as a young boy. This evil emaciated woman has lured Ku into a dungeon, saying that she is in great pain and needs a healer's help. Appealing to Ku's pride, she adds that he is young and has much to share and he agrees, freeing the shackles at her wrists and feet.

When the final restraint is off, the crone leaps toward Ku and plunges her bony hand, her flowing red-silk sleeve fluttering behind, into his chest and extracts something— he's wasn't quite sure what. The removal brings about a pain within Ku, which is so deep it travels beyond his flesh and far into ancient portions of his soul. He feels helpless, powerless against this invasion. Within a blink of an eye, she holds a glowing aquamarine jewel in her veined hand, which he instantly understands is the embodiment of all his healing abilities

Then the crone's body begins to stretch, her face becomes a gnarled, knotted, unrecognizable mess. Ku watches as the frail woman morphs into a distended, flabby, slimy mass. Putrid brown ooze pours from what he can only guess are its eyes and mouth. A stench emanates from five large boils, which spurt frothy, yellow pus. The feeling that he gets when this monster unveils itself is almost worse that the disgusting visuals. Ku is overcome with despair, terror, and unfathomable loss. The assault on his senses freezes him on the spot.

While this scene unfolds in her mind, Hillary's chest tightens. Her screams stick in her throat. She wants to go back in time and help poor Ku and as her desire to come to the little boy's aid intensifies, Hillary sees a vortex open which extends from her feet to an abyss far below. An invisible force begins to suck her back in time, back to Ku and to that frightening scene. As it does so, the crone appears in the center of the vortex and speaks to Hillary:

"Never mind about Ku, you have bigger fish to fry."

The crone flashes a picture of Heidi and Molly, clinging to each other and crying as they hover in darkness. Just below them is the Island of Japan.

"Now, I have your family for safe keeping."

Fighting for her life, Hillary summons all her strength to yank her mind back to the present, to this hot, dark dungeon. Without a doubt she knows the evil old crone is behind her, Molly's and Heidi's otherworldly imprisonment, and Hillary strengthens her resolve to avenge all the unthinkable destruction the crone has caused on this earth. Thoughts and images of the crone's blob personae jab into Hillary's brain as she writhes and jerks about trying to break free. In doing so, she manages to free one arm and waves it madly trying to find something on which to grab.

With one last burst of energy, she pushes through a dark membrane, shearing it with her bare hand, and the stuck scream finally escapes from her throat, "Aaaaaaaaaaaahhhhh."

Hillary sits up, gasping and heaving, shards of light almost cut through her corneas. She sputters in the blinding bright lights, which the evil crone/blob, she assumes, uses for her tortuous interrogations. Ready for battle with the evil force, Hillary lets out a battle cry. A blob-like form hovers over her, the undersides of its tentacles glistening white, with one large glistening red suction cup in the center.. Proud that her voice is back in full form, she screams, "You are a wicked, vile, noxious force of humanity. I am here to speak for all those who were unfortunate enough to incur your wrath. Aaaaaaarrrrrggghhhhhhh!!"

Gulping in the fresh air and blinking in the bright light, Hillary braces for the impact of an evil blast of energy.

"Excuse me, Miss. You must have been dreaming." A perfectly coiffed, young woman's face with blinding white teeth comes into view, and then she pats Hillary's arm showing off her blood red manicured fingers.

Hillary lowers her gaze to a crumpled dark blanket on an airplane seat—her dank prison. She takes in the young flight attendant's long white arm and bright red nail polish—the glistening white tentacles with a red suction cup. The attendant sniffs officiously using the toe of her black pump to free the brake of the drink cart she had been pushing—the source of the fearsome death rattle.

Hillary, completely disoriented, moves her gaze around the packed plane. Rows and rows of occupants all gape at her matted curls, which stick to her forehead. The black blanket now lies in a puddle around her ankles.

After what seems to be an eternity, everyone except an elderly woman seated across the aisle return to their books or computers. The woman examines Hillary unapologetically from matted bedhead to disheveled flip-flops.

"Um…Where am I." Her voice hoarse from screaming, Hillary whispers to the curious woman.

"I'm not sure where you are, but I am on a plane to Orange County." The woman's soft, wrinkly mouth turns up and her eyes twinkle.

A jolt of recognition zings through Hillary as she looks down at her right hand. Her fuchsia fingernails are clutching the blue pleather armrests of her airplane seat. She runs her hand over her face, her legs and her hair. She is back in her own body! Then Hillary glances out of the window and sees the familiar structures of the John Wayne Airport and just beyond it, the glistening Pacific Ocean. The pilot announces the flight's end. She is on her way back home to Los Tardos, California!

I manage to move my wrists into a position in which the thick leather restraints are not cutting into my flesh. However, there is no escaping the distinct pain caused by the acupuncturist's sadistic methods. I've had acupuncture before. Usually, the needles are inserted with a quick tap and the experience is relatively painless. If it is necessary, I've had acupuncturists turn the needle once or twice. This man's use of needles is more like "acu-torture." The insertion is not just a quick tap, it is more like a sharp jab and the turning of the needles, well, his average so far is eight or ten times.

Once again, I close my eyes, praying for peace and freedom from this horrific place. I must believe that some good will come of this. In fact, it almost seems imperative that I find healing within the pain.

A memory seeps in and I follow it, if only to escape my present discomfort for a brief moment.

"Mina?" My mother is touching my forehead with a wet cloth and she looks concerned.

I am five years old and I lie on a bed made of an old feed sack stuffed with straw. I have contracted an illness that no one, not even our village healer can diagnose, and my mother has separated me from my brothers and sisters for fear that I might be contagious.

My eyes flutter open and I ask her, "Did I die?"

Creases of worry cover her face as she shakes her head, unable to speak. Wiry gray hairs have broken free from her smooth black braid and move around her face with the breeze wafting through the open door. I've been this way for a month with no change. Finally, she tells my brother to call on our local witch doctor. She never would send for him because his methods are unorthodox and often harsh, but under the circumstances, she feels she must.

Truth be told, despite my feeling awful, I am thrilled because this is the most tenderness my mother has shown me in my entire life. I relish her gentle strokes and touches on my cheek and revel in her obvious fear. This deep concern permeates every cell of my being and makes me feel like I'm inside her. It is the first time I have been fully aware that I can feel emotions of others as if they are my own.

The witch doctor enters my room with a flourish and asks my mother to step away from the bed. He is a small man. His head reaches just over the mattress, and with his ceremonial mask, he resembles a gremlin or gnome. His red robe is tied with a wide gold brocade sash and he carries an animal skin cinched at the top.

Intoning a deep rumbling chant, he slowly moves around my bed. As he arrives at my side, he reaches into the back and pulls out metal bells and begins to shake them over my head and torso, then over my feet.

He returns the bells back to their dark home, deep within his animal skin tote, then places his hands about a foot over my body and appears to feel or sense something. Directing my mother and siblings who had gathered in the bedroom doorway to move far, he gathers up a deep breath, pulls his hands in a circular motion at the top of my head and with a loud whooshing exhale, sends whatever negativity or anomaly he felt in my aura away from my body and out the open door.

I feel a chill as he gathers more energy from around my body and says, "You are so easy to work on. Your energy is not difficult to move at all. Soon you will feel much better."

My mother looks drawn and weak as she watches the witch doctor work. Sunlight catches wayward gray hairs and lights them creating a halo all around her crown, her ears and her neck.

After one more pass of this energy, my fever is gone and I do feel something—naked. Not just unclothed, but unprotected. I feel exposed and my mother's fear seems to have burrowed into my soul so that I no longer can tell if it is my fear or hers.

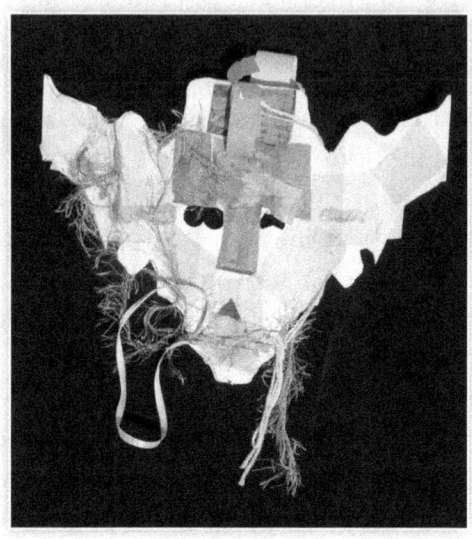

Before he leaves, the witch doctor pulls his ceremonial mask off and tucks it under his arm, gazes intensely into my eyes and says, "Iron does not age, it gains patina. In its own way, it transforms through alchemy."

I had no idea that this man had summed up my entire future with these words. From the outside, "patina" is a beautiful transformation. No one asks the iron if it wants to patina or if the patina hurts. From the outside, anything can look beautiful. The experience from the inside is a completely different story.

CHAPTER IV

Clear Sky

Ritual: Mother Love
Element: Silver
Planet: Moon

---

*Sit in the light of the full moon. It doesn't matter if you are inside
or out, just make sure that the moon's bright light bathes you in
its gorgeous glow.*

*Imagine that the full moon is the Great Mother's belly, full to the
point of bursting with unconditional love, abundance and wealth
beyond measure. Now, imagine that the full moon's rays have the
power to fill your body with nourishing, fulfilling goodness. Breathe
in these gifts. See the Great Mother holding you in her embrace as you
are lovingly given everything you've ever wanted on this earth. Each
gift she imparts and every particle of light contains a reminder of
that which you already possess: love, respect, healing, and wealth. See
those gifts (and any others which are unique to you).*

When you have had your fill, thank the moon—the Great Mother—and see yourself full to the point of bursting with unconditional love, abundance and wealth beyond measure.

All the treasures for which you search are accessible. You are worthy of receiving these gifts any time you wish.

Hillary scans the silver line of the horizon separating the deep, dark blue of the sparkling Pacific from the blue-gray sky. Her mind reels from her jarring metaphysical travels and she tries to create a reasonable explanation for how she was transported back into her physical body and to a plane heading to her home in Los Tardos.

If the crone was going to go to all this trouble, she must want something from her. But what? And why not send her to Japan instead of back home to the small Southern California town where she grew up?

Then another thought occurs to her: What if this has all been a dream? The hypnotherapy recording she used for her fear of flying could have created hallucinations. The last two weeks could definitely be explained away as an otherworldly illusion brought on by stress.

Wearily, Hillary sinks into her seat. It seems like a lifetime ago that she was on the plane to Honolulu. Although just two weeks have passed, she does her best to piece together her journey. She didn't aim to solve mysteries or save Hawaii, but when Moa appeared to her, Hillary had a feeling she was destined to set aside her modest vacation plans and, instead, follow Moa's instructions.

She really needs some rest. Perhaps a nice nap will do her good. Closing her eyes, Hillary savors the feeling of being in her own skin. Her clothes create a slight pressure on her shoulders and legs and the nubbly bottom of her flip-flops feels rough against the soles of her feet. She lowers her chin to her chest and senses the pull of her neck muscles as she inhales deeply to relax her body. She's never really enjoyed flying. This deep breathing exercise was suggested to her by a hypnotherapist she visited a couple of months before her trip to Hawaii to quell her terrifying thoughts of shearing through the clouds at high speed thousands of feet above the Earth.

Hillary can feel the elderly woman across the aisle staring at her unabashedly and she through closed eyes, focuses her attention straight ahead as she wills her body to relax. The plane shudders. Breathe deep, she remembers the kind hypnotherapist saying.

The plane bumps three times heavily. The captain instructs all passengers to return to their seats and requests that the flight attendants be seated as well.

Eyes snapping open, she digs frantically in her backpack for her hypnotherapy recording, Hillary can see the elderly woman out of the corner of her eye. It is uncomfortable enough to experience a fear of flying, but to be observed doing so is almost too much to bear. Much to her disappointment, she cannot find her iPod. Despite doing her best to imagine waves of love and light flow into her body, the plane bounces along as if it is a bus with no shock absorbers on a rutted country road. Hillary is about to tell the woman to mind her own business when the plane suddenly drops.

Passengers scream, drinks and snacks soar up and over neighboring seats and for the second time today, Hillary screams, too.

A hand on hers stops Hillary's voice, then the old lady says, "My daddy used to say, 'Cursing the inevitable is like pulling the rip cord on a parachute before you jump out of the plane. Not helpful, potentially lethal.' What would your daddy say?"

Hillary clutches at the soft loose flesh on the woman's hand and closes her eyes. It feels as if she is the only tether to reality and she's not going to let go—rip cord reference or not. As Hillary looks deep into the woman's watery blue eyes, she is drawn in and through them. It's as if this woman has created a portal to comfort and relaxation. All she has to do is allow it to draw her into its depths. But, something stops her. More fear clogs the flow to calmness.

The old woman keeps her hand where it is, she is committed to her cause—it's almost like her touch embraces Hillary's whole being. Again, Hillary is pulled into the woman's eyes but she bumps up against an immovable, impenetrable force. The clog materializes into a question: What would her daddy say? It is as if this question put out to Hillary has become a real, physical manifestation and Hillary finds herself clutching her father's hand. In this freefalling, moment her father is sitting across from her instead of the old woman and he says, "The only person you have to answer to is yourself, Hillary. If you fear life, it will give you fear. Don't look to me for those precious, desired answers, because, in the end, I will only be to blame for what they are not."

It is as if time stretches and Hillary is finally able to breathe in expansiveness, openness and the immovable force begins to become opaque. She thinks, what if I have all the answers? Both terrifying and mind-blowing, Hillary's fear disappears within the confines of these thoughts. Suddenly, the blockage is removed and Hillary zips through the portal and in a flash of white light, she finds herself back in her seat the old woman's veined hand still pressed against her own,

The old woman gives a gentle smile, slips her hand away from Hillary's and folds her hands in her lap. She gives a knowing nod and wink as the plane levels off and flies smoothly for two full minutes before the pilot announces, with great apologies, that they encountered 'clear air turbulence.'

"Well, now I've heard it all…" Hillary mutters to herself. "A perfectly clear sky and we hit turbulence?"

"Nothing can hurt you more than your mind allows." The old woman says before turning to look out the window away from Hillary.

The orange red glow of the setting sun comes in slivers through the barred window. My mother has yet to return to take me home.

Since there is no clock and I do not have a timepiece it is impossible to know how long I've been in the dank treatment room. Sounds come from the street below—screeching brakes, the high pitched wail of sirens and shopkeepers rolling their front gates as they lock up for the evening.

Sadness floods my forehead, my eyes and my ears, working its way down as a shadow covers a playground. I remember my father as a kind, gentle man, who taught me how to clear the chicken coop, mark cattle for sale and ward off animal poachers. His teaching style was by example and one incident plays through my addled, pincushion brain.

We were walking two goats to market to sell the milk. I was chosen to go with him because my mother was, as always, busy with my older brothers and sisters. It was a beautiful spring morning and the dew created sparkling diamonds on the path to the market. My favorite part of every journey was when my father would begin to quote ancient texts. His favorite was "*Seiko udoku*" which literally translates as: Clear sky, cultivate; rainy, reading. What the saying means is "Farm when it's sunny, read when it rains."

My father loved to read. When all the work was done, we could always find him tucked away in a corner with his nose in any sort of book. Most of the books we owned were passed down from my great-grandfather and grandfather.

As we neared the entrance to the market, a smartly dressed man approached my father and bowed deeply. My father returned this respectful gesture and the man launched into a long speech about how his family owned hundreds cattle in the northern city and would like to expand. He continued talking as others passed us and, finally, when my father politely declined, the man's demeanor changed. He yelled at my father and began gesturing wildly. It seemed that this man might harm us; yet, as his anger escalated, my father remained calm. The man reached into his breast pocket and pulled out a knife. This is what my father would call *seiten no heki-reki* or a "thunderclap from a clear sky."

But, his reaction stays with me to this day. With a nod of his head, my father simply said, "No, san."

Just as the wind changes its course, my father's words cause the would-be assailant to move away from us. He turned and walked away, continuing his rant, but moving along down the lane and far from us.

Plodding on, the delay by the strange man causing us to lose valuable time with customers, my father muttered, "*Baka was shinanakya naoranai*" or "You can't fix stupid."

Now lying still, needles protruding from my body, my leaden heart feels like it will drop out of my chest onto the table beneath me as I relive my father's funeral. The air was crisp and clear on that autumn morning. We had no money for a horse drawn carriage, but instead put his body in a hole dug by my uncles and brothers. I could see my oldest brother's breath wafting on the air as he read one of my father's favorite passages:

When a man in the beginning of his life is ignorant of everything, he has no scruples, finds no obstacles, no inhibitions. But after a while he starts to learn, and becomes timid, cautious, and begins to feel something choking in his mind, which prevents him from going ahead as he used to before he had any learning. Learning is needed, but the point is not to become its slave. You must be its master, so that you can use it when you want it.
- Yagyu Munemori (1571-1646)

I inherited my father's love of details, becoming breathless over dewdrops on blades of grass, and the like. My father would stare for hours on end at a spider spinning a web and I, in turn, would watch him watching. There was something so beautiful in his awe of nature, of life, of humanity. It was a quiet awe, but it was a sincere wonderment, nonetheless.

That day, amid the whispers and tears, I heard the words separately from different conversations and unsuspecting people—sudden, collapse and weak heart. I remember standing at my father's gravesite after everyone had gone home and watching a beetle scurry across the freshly filled-in dirt of his grave with the bleak wish I could be in there with him.

My mind returns to the dank room and the smell of the leather straps restraining my arms and legs. Large drops of rain begin to hit the copper rain gutter in rhythm as another cloudburst travels overhead. I hear the rumble of the thunder, the vast quiet between the enormous water drops splashing against the metal drainpipes and the anticipation of a deluge as the spacing in between the raindrops lessens. This is a nature-induced symphony, which I know my father would love.

There is no more space between the drops and the storm sounds more like giant pails of water being poured out onto the pavement, the cars and the trashcans. This can't be real, I think. Surely, my mother will come back. I've lost track of how long it's been since I've seen her and I desperately try to conjure her up in my memory. The slight curve of her brow as she scrubbed and clanged the pans, the glistening gray strands of hair that would peek out of her braid and the gentle nod she would give me upon first laying eyes on me in the morning. Her scent was sharp and bitter, like a lightening storm mixed with ginger root and it was the smell of my home, of my love, of my mother.

But nothing changes the fact that I am here, alone and she is not here. The pressure of envisioning her absence, desperately imagining makes me wonder if I am the cause of her leaving. Did I do something? Maybe she is angry? I beg forgiveness from this made-up mother. I weep for myself. Suddenly, I see her turn her back on me and walk away. How, on earth, could a mother abandon her daughter? A fury builds inside my head sending pulsing beams of rage into every cell of my body and that is when it happens. I feel a snap deep inside my soul, a resounding rip of such enormous proportions and permanence that I know I will never be the same.

Suddenly, I am walking, unfettered, through glistening, silvery, wet streets of the city. Away from the treatment room, my rendered self goes, out into the storm without a care, far from the dread, the suffering and the torture—I am free!

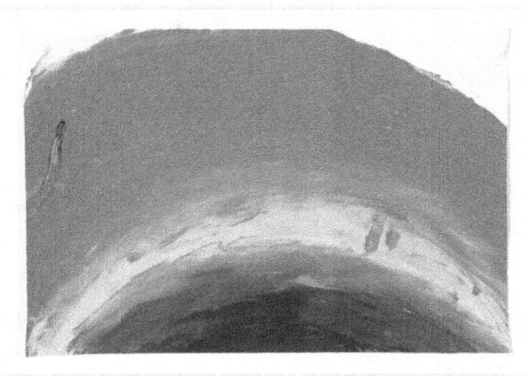

CHAPTER V

Insight

Ritual: Inner Sight
Element: Gold
Planet: Sun

*At dawn's first light, face East and say the following
words three times:*

I am willing to trust my own insight.
*Imagine the sun's golden light permeating your body, releasing
any negative thoughts, fears or worries. See them dissolve and
imagine that they are replaced with a new positive thought, a new
perspective and a confident feeling.*

Hillary's face is pressed to the window, peering out into the clouds. From the aisle next to her she senses the old woman throwing glances her way, and a little tingle goes through her. She hates being observed.

The pilot announces the plane's descent and she eagerly wonders what adventure awaits her on the ground. Somehow, this flight has calmed her nerves and strengthened her resolve to find her sister and niece and reunite their Ka with their bodies.

Gathering up her backpack, she smiles at the old woman across the aisle who gives her a nod and scoots out of her seat as she disembarks.

Hillary makes her way to baggage claim, hoping that her luggage will be ready for her on the carousel. The carousel is idle and she must wait for the bags to descend and as she does so, a pang hits her when she remembers how she left Los Tardos when she first went to Hawaii.

The trip was a high school graduation gift from her parents. Her heart drops as she imagines what her reunion will be like with her father.

"I know he's behind this." Anger causes Hillary's chest to tighten as she recalls muttering to herself mere hours before her flight to Hawaii. She had a sneaking suspicion that he had taken her iPod for safe keeping.

Her father always believed that his daughter would be much better off if she faced her fear of flying without anyone else's help.

Hillary had scoured every bag, drawer and her purse several times before confronting her father. "Okay. Where is it?"

"You're fine." Her father was sitting, as always, at his workbench in the family garage, tying fly-fishing lures. Looking up from his work he continued, "No daughter of mine should have to rely on schlocky pseudoscience to get through a simple flight. You can do this on your own. Here." He presented her with a carefully prepared bag including two packs of peppermint gum, a paper sack—in case of hyperventilation—a copy of the Magazine *Modern Teen* and a Snickers bar—to eat as a reward when she made it to the end. Then he added, "You're a strong girl. You'll be fine."

Frustrated by the misunderstanding and fueled by fear of her impending flight, Hillary had flown into a rage, "Yes, I am strong AND I want my iPod. Now!"

"C'mon, Hil." Her father chuckled. "Surely you can tough it out. You'll thank me when it's over."

Those words broke the dam that held back every upset about being misunderstood during her high school years. After her rant, her father unearthed the missing iPod from beneath a pile of old *National Geographic* magazines and tossed it at Hillary in disgust. "It's just a crutch. Eventually, you're going to have to face your fears and when that day comes I hope your iPod is charged."

Hearing the noise, her mother had come in to the garage just as Hillary let loose a string of obscenities. Anger spewed from every part of her as Hillary screamed at her parents. She berated them for all of her loneliness and angst and said she would be out of the house as soon as her trip ended. With that, she stormed out of the house and took the city bus to the airport.

Hillary is jolted back to the present as the carousel starts up and bags begin to drop down the ramp from above. Surprisingly, hers is the first bag dropped.

"When has that ever happened?" She mutters to herself as she grabs her large suitcase, and heaves it over the lip of the carousel lifting the long handle and rolling toward the exit.

She's got just enough money to take an airport shuttle home and she heads in the direction of a local shuttle company stand.

"Ride, miss?" An extremely tall gentleman with shaggy dark hair and a curly mustache nods toward his black sedan. He has a nametag pinned to his lapel which says Mr. Amaranth Najit, Cartel Car Service.

Although both the sedan and driver look official, Hillary is wary of taking a car from an unknown source.

"No thanks." She brushes past the man and stands in line at the shuttle stand.

The shuttle has not yet arrived, so she takes her place at the end of the line next to a woman pushing a stroller. As she waits, she scans over the people scurrying to and fro. The shuttle bus pulls up and the line shortens as people step aboard. Hillary fishes in her handbag for her wallet, but, it has disappeared!

She looks up just as Mr. Najit catches her eye and gives her a nod, waving her wallet in the air

Why, that sneak! She mutters to herself as she makes her way out of the shuttle line, across the crowded street and stomps over to confront the smiling driver.

"How dare you!" Hillary snatches her wallet from him and whirls around just in time to see the shuttle bus leave.

"Now you really do need a ride." The driver bows to her and motions to his sedan, "Right this way, miss."

"No thank you. I don't ride with thieves! What I ought to do is report you immediately!" She turns to wave at a nearby police officer, but stops in her track by the next thing she hears.

"Are you so sure about that Hillary Hause?" asks Mr. Najit in an amused tone.

"How do you know m…" She looks deep into the driver's eyes. Something is familiar about them.

"What are you doing here, that's what I'd like to know. You should be in Japan right now. Shouldn't you?" The driver lets out an unusual giggle.

"It can't be…" Hillary steps closer to the driver and looks him up and down.

"Moa? Is that *you*?"

I am unsure of how it has happened, nonetheless, I am free!

The street is slick with rain and each drop looks like a jewel falling from the sky. My breath comes out in puffs from the cold, but I'm so exhilarated. I don't feel it as I stop on the first street corner, abutted with trashcans and bags piled upon one another awaiting the morning pickup. I stop to ponder the possibilities. Where to go?

Then a voice from the past brushes through my hair and tickles my ear. It is my father's voice. I remember him waking us and ushering me and my brothers and sisters out into the dark night to watch a meteor shower. As we watched the gorgeous night show of silver shooting stars against the velvet black sky, my father said, "Nebulas cannot be seen if you look at them straight, but can only be seen if you see them from your periphery. Imagine what else we could see if we saw it from a different perspective."

A rush of wind passes through me, nearly knocking me over, pressing me to choose a direction. If I go right, I can head back toward the village in which I was raised. I can only imagine the fate which would await me if I wandered back to my family. Left will take me to the sea and perhaps a boat in which I might travel to other countries and meet new people. Straight ahead will lead deep into the heart of the city and all of its mysterious underworld life.

Another rush of wind pushes me forward and I first jog, then run through the streets toward my new life—my new adventure.

Not another soul is outside during the gale. I wander into an alley just to get away from the knife-sharp gusts, which pull at my clothes and yank at my feet. Is the wind deterring me or guiding me?

Then I see a light glowing from a basement apartment. Inside, a young woman sits reading a book, knitting a shawl by a large small fireplace. Surely she will help me find my way out of this unusual situation and offer me shelter for the night.

Moving closer to the window, I crouch down to make sure it is safe and see the most incredible sight. At her feet are little girls, six of them, all about my age and size. All are wrapped in shawls and are snuggled up around the fire. Each girl looks completely content and satisfied, and it is all I can do to keep from skipping down the steps and doing a dance as I lift the frigid iron doorknocker. But, I take pause before I knock and look, once again, at the girls nestled in warmth and comfort. What if this is not real? A shard of wind jabs my back and I push away my fears as I tap the knocker three times.

"Hello, Mina. I've been expecting you!" The woman's voice is so soothing I don't even wonder at how she knows my name or why she has been expecting me. Her kind attention warms my heart and softens my frozen-stiff fingers and toes.

"Come now, and sit by the fire."

Within moments, I have a cup of steaming hot tea thrust into my cold hands, and I am seated closest to the fire. Next to the woman is an ornate table, which stands out in this simply furnished room, on which is an empty mug and a single sheet of paper. The print is way too small to read, and, besides, my attention is turned to the fire and the tea and the warm glow that seems to be over everything.

I move toward the group and select the last empty pillow in the circle of girls and attempt to settle in. Now that I can get a closer look at the girls around the fire, I notice something odd. Each one wears the same expression of vacant surprise and bewilderment as I feel. I wonder if each girl has been plucked from a violent situation and found her way here to absolute comfort just as I did.

Bathed by the firelight, I absorb the beguiling civility of the soft silk cushion on which I am seated. I'll take just a moment to rest, I think, and then I'll be on my way.

"Of course, you can choose to stay as long as you wish, Mina." The woman does not look up from her knitting. "But know that there are comforts here which can not be attained anywhere else." As she says these words, the words on the paper next to her become crystal clear. At the top of the page are the words, "Apprenticeship Contract." I begin to read:

"I, Minamoto, do hereby waive all my rights in exchange for food and shelter."

Why on earth would I sign such a ridiculous contract? I chuckle to myself. Suddenly, a jolt of fear shocks my core. What if I am wrong? Perhaps if I go, I'll encounter great harm. This thought grows within me and emerges in my mind's eye as a frightening scene.

I see myself leaving this place and the moment I step out onto the street, a crone with sharp, bony fingers appears, buries her hand into my chest and steals my soul, my very essence. She holds the glistening mass up to a streetlight, lets out a shrill cackle and then vanishes. As I wander the streets, attempting to find food and shelter, no one will take me in because they are frightened by my presence. I am a soulless person and I emit an odorless stench of desperation so abysmal that no one dare come to my aid. This, I hear a voice deep within my body say, is my future.

A chill runs through me and I pull the warm mug close to my chest. The icy fingers continue to shoot up my spine, through the base of my skull and down my forehead. Before I know it, I am more chilled than I was when I first entered this place.

"Of course," the woman repeats, "It is completely your choice."

If the girls surrounding us heard her, none reacted or said a word. In that moment I did not fear for my life. I feared for my soul.

CHAPTER VI
Embodiment

Ritual: Embodiment
Element: Silver
Planet: Pluto

Within your body, there is a core of light. It is in that light, that you may realign and rejuvenate your soul and mind with your body. Sit in a quiet place where you will not be interrupted. Breath deeply for ten breaths and imagine that a column of light runs through your body with the top of the column at the crown of your head and the bottom going through the base of your spine.

Now, imagine that this light column has the power to center any parts of your self that are out of alignment, physical, mental or spiritual. These parts can be energetic or material and this light column will release, call back, clear and strengthen your body, mind, spirit and soul. Your words have the power to direct this healing to occur.

Say the following:
I bring in protection as I align all parts of myself with my core essence. I release all that is not connected to my divine purpose and shore up my core strength. I bring in flexibility, openness, stability and love and ask that my body be healed with high vibrational Source energy. We are one.

Continue breathing and allow the light column to do its work. Drink plenty of water throughout the day and get plenty of rest after this ritual.

"Ha! Ha! Tee hee, hee, hee." Mr. Najit jumps up and down on his tiptoes giggling like a little girl. "I love to do this! Hi, Hil."

The sight of the enormous man behaving in such an incongruous way is hilarious, and Hillary is so relieved to see her long lost friend, Moa, she drops her bag and lunges forward, wrapping her arms around the large man's torso. "Oh Moa! I've missed you so much! Molly and Heidi are trapped and the crone, she put me in a plane, but I have my body now but they don't…"

"I know, I know. Remember, I'm a spirit again."

"I see that." Hillary says warmly, "You're back to your 'temporary housing' again."

"Hey," Moa says defensively, "he was on a break, taking a nap in his car, and totally agreed with my plan."

"Really? Where do you find these people?" Hillary picks up her purse and nods to the large suitcase, "Would you mind? It's awfully heavy."

"Sure, no problem." Moa picks up the suitcase like it is a backpack, pulls a remote out of a back pocket and presses the trunk release button.

"Thanks," Hillary says as the suitcase lands in the trunk with a thump.

Moa bows deeply as she opens the sedan's door and says with mock subservience, "Allow me, miss."

Hillary giggles and steps into the luxurious black sedan and inhales the new car smell. "Nice car. You chose well."

"Nothing but the best for m' lady." Moa continues her driver charade then dissolves into snorts of laughter. When she recovers she adjusts her cap and says, "Okay. Where to? I am much better with directions when I'm up there." She looks up through the open sunroof.

"Home, um, what's your name?" Hillary glances at the license posted on the car's dashboard, "Amaranth. Just go straight out here and follow the road to the airport exit. I'll tell you where to go." She settles back and takes in the opulence of the luxury car. "So when did you learn how to drive? I thought you left earth when you were seven?"

The car lurches forward. "Actually, I never did…" Moa hits the gas and shoots out of the airport pickup lane, weaving to and fro. Finally, Moa jams on the brakes at a red light. "How am I doing so far?"

"I think I'd better drive. Stay there," Hillary hops out and opens the driver side door as the light changes and the cars behind them honk.

"Just a minute. Can't you see we're switching?" Moa hops in the back and stretches out taking up the entire back seat. "Hey, this really is a swanky auto."

Hillary looks into the rear view mirror and chuckles. "So where have you been? The last we saw, you were with Ku"

"It's kind of hard to explain, but let's say, I was consulting with my 'team.'"

"You have an entire team? Well, we sure could have used your help. Didn't you hear us when we called out for you? Molly, Heidi and I got separated from our bodies, then got stuck using the Iron Shinto to transport our-selves to Japan in an attempt to find them. I have a feeling the crone had something to do with it and she brought me back here, too.

"It feels so much better being back in my body. I don't know how you do it." Hillary takes a deep breath ready to unload, but Moa interrupts.

"Hil. I am sorry I couldn't come. It's kind of compli-cated. Right now, though, we must get Heidi and Molly out of their disembodied stasis as soon as possible. I know what the crone wants and she's asking you to do work for her that she needs to do herself."

"But why is she holding us hostage?"

"She's afraid. Right now, she is under the illusion of powerlessness. That can make people do all kinds of crazy things. They energetically thrash and flail about causing great harm to others."

"I don't know, Moa. She seems pretty directed and clear about wanting to harm us."

"Oh, that's what she wants you to think. Desperation can do that. What you must do is promise me you'll not fall into fear. Can you promise me that, Hil?" Moa looks earnestly at Hillary.

"Of course." She turns onto a highway and immediately hits traffic, "Oh great! I forgot about freeway traffic."

Hillary takes the opportunity to take in Moa's current "housing." She'd explained before that, upon agreement, spirits can take over any human body and "drive" it around for a while. Then an idea hits her, "Hey, Moa what if Molly and Heidi found some temporary housing of their own. But..." before she can finish, Moa interrupts.

"A great idea, Hil!"

"But do you think they'll know how to do it? What if there is an accident?

"There is always a chance they could get trapped in their host body." Moa shakes her head. "I don't know if it's worth the risk when they are scattered around up there."

"What do you mean, 'scattered'?" Hillary says.

"While you were up there with them, didn't you feel strange?"

"Well...yes." Hilary shrugs

"That is because when your Ka separates from your body, it expands. Essentially, it has no container, so it expands over a wide area. Did you notice the strange way you sounded? That was sound bending around the dimensions. In most cases a disembodied Ka can last a maximum of forty-eight hours."

"Then what?" Hillary's stomach drops.

"Well, I'm sorry to say, the Ka will completely dissipate."

"What do you mean?"

"Will you stop asking me what I mean?" Moa shakes her head. "They are going to be fine, I will make sure. For now, you've got some work to do. You've got to get home and figure out what that crone needs so we can help her move on. She's stuck, and she firmly believes you three are her only way out."

"That's not true?" Hillary says.

"Not entirely." Moa says. "Think about it this way. We're all, I mean all of us, in this together. So we help each other whether we know it or not. But the kind of help this crone is asking for would mean that you would sacrifice your gifts, those essential parts of you, for her ascension.

"I don't want to help her! I can't stand her! All I want is to get my sister and niece back here safe."

"Unfortunately, she will not let them go until she gets what she wants."

"Can't you stop her?" Hillary grips the steering wheel in frustration.

"No. You all are in a situation in which I cannot intervene. The best I can do is guide you and them. She has created an odd distortion chamber in which all who approach her are forced to do her bidding. She has created her own version of hell."

"What are you saying? You mean hell isn't real?" Hillary's knuckles are white on her steering wheel.

"No, hell is an illusion created by humans who distance themselves from the light. You have got to beat her at her own game. I know I can help you do that, but we've only got about forty hours to get them back safely." Moa says.

Sick of inching along in the bumper to bumper traffic, Hillary pulls onto the shoulder, "To beat her at her own game, we are going to have to break some rules. May as well get started now!"

Making certain no one is ahead of her, she presses the accelerator. They zip by about fifty cars when Hillary hears a siren and looks back. "Oh, no!"

A police car pulls up close behind them and Hillary slows down, then stops.

"Breaking rules does have its consequences." Moa smiles.

"Yes it does. Now how are we going to explain me driving your car!" Hillary hisses as Moa's smile fades.

The Apprenticeship Contract sits on the table in front of me, and the warmth of the fire gives me little comfort as I squirm on my silk cushion and search for my answer. The girls—all with matching half smiles, dark brown hair, sitting cross-legged with right leg over left, hands clasped on laps, looking straight ahead with dilated black pupils—offer nothing in the way of support as I press myself to decide—to stay or to go.

Here among a group of girls my age, I would face an unknown future. By the bewildered looks on the girl's faces surrounding me, I understand that, at least in part, my future would be one of compliance and complacency. However, the scene in which I imagined leaving this place still plays fresh in my mind. I can almost feel the tight soreness in my chest where the crone's bony hand penetrated, then extracted my essence and the gaping hole within my body wherein my soul once lived.

I am certain this scene did not happen, but the threat is so real, I feel more and more that it is destined to occur if I step outside the confines of the "safe" environment.

Desperately, I peruse the room once more for a clue as to how I should make my overwhelmingly difficult decision. Exactly why the need for making my choice is so important, I do not know. However, with each minute that passes, my chest seems to tighten a little more and, although I'm not sure how I know this, I believe that a decision will quell my fear within.

"I'll make it easy for you," the knitting woman senses my ambivalence. "I'll give you a job working for me. That way, you'll earn your place in our little..." she searches deep within her yarn, looking more and more like Madame Defarge in *A Tale of Two Cities*, her eyes scanning between loops and purls for the words and then satisfied, she looks directly into my eyes and purrs, "enclave."

Amazed, I watch as the wording on the contract dissolves, then reappears with the woman's new words:

"I, Minamoto, hereby agree to work in exchange for food and shelter."

Her gaze cements an idea in my mind: Sign on with the knitting woman and you, Mina, will be safe for eternity—safe from the unknown outside world. I nod in agreement and see my signature magically appear on the contract. For the moment, I am content with my decision. But that feeling is gone as quickly as it settles. All of the girls awaken and begin talking with one another animatedly. Each girl begins to gain an identity.

The two girls to my right have orange skin, purple shoulder length hair and matching red hair bows and talk simultaneously. "Welcome!" they say in unison.

I smile at them and before I can speak, the face of the girl who is seated directly in front of me begins to change. Her dark brown eyebrows grow together into a caterpillar-like mass above her eyes, which creates a permanent scowl and her skin turns a dark green. My smile fades as she glares into my eyes, "Welcome," she says, without a trace of a smile. "Go get Her some water."

The Red Bows point to the Unibrow and in a show of solidarity toward their scowling friend say, "Listen to her. She got here first."

Feeling slightly threatened by this strange girl and her orders—after all, I work for the knitting woman, not this unibrowed creature—I look over at the woman who continues her knitting and rocking routine. She doesn't look thirsty.

Perhaps I should use the direct approach and ask her myself. I do my best to get her attention. First, I clear my throat. After no reaction from Her, I rise and address the knitting woman, "Excuse me. Would you like some water?"

The Unibrow snickers behind me as knitting woman ignores my question.

"Pardon," my voice begins to quaver, "I...uh...Do you want some water?"

"See?" The Unibrow lets out a self-satisfied breath and continues, "Now go get the water."

The girls have become a tittering, clucking bunch of chickens and I can hear their comments as they point at me:

"She's not in charge."

"I don't like her."

"Why not?"

"She's weak."

Bowing under the pressure of appearing to do my job incorrectly, I feel my face redden at the thought of others talking about me. It appears that a new job qualification, not mentioned on the agreement, has surfaced—mind reader. Hoping that the knitting woman is indeed thirsty and is in need of water, I walk over to a pitcher and grab a clean mug from a nearby shelf. Worried that I may spill the water on my trip back to the knitting woman, I fill it half way and turn to make my way back to Her.

The Unibrow sneers, "Can you believe it? She only filled the glass half way! Of all the incompetence."

Deeply ashamed, I set the glass on a table next to Her and return to my silk cushion.

"You didn't put a coaster under the glass? Tsk, tsk, tsk."

Clucks and chatters follow Unibrow's comments.

"How incompetent."

"Why did She hire her?"

"I have no idea."

All the while, as the comments continue, the woman keeps rocking and knitting, knitting and rocking.

I reason with myself that perhaps this girl, her unibrow growing thicker and her skin greener with each interaction, would like to team up. Perhaps she doesn't know that we can actually help one another and so I choose to ignore the titters and snide comments and say to her, "Listen. We can work as a team." Her face never changes expression as I lay out a plan, "How about if we take turns? I can get the water once and you can get it the next time."

"Sure." The Unibrow replies blankly.

Hours go by, the chill that had once permeated my bones is nearly gone and I seem to be making friends. In fact, the Bows begin to pay me compliments by saying I am lucky to work for someone so important like Her. "She is very powerful and you have been chosen exclusively to work with Her. That must make you incredibly special."

I can feel Unibrow's ire with each positive word the Bows direct toward me.

So, I turn toward the girl to my left, who, up until now, I haven't spoken with directly. The girl wears purple glasses and has a toothy grin.

"Hello," I try to smile through my nervousness. "Would you like to play a game?"

"Sure." I think it is impossible that the girl's smile can get any bigger, but it does, "I love games!"

A low rumble begins within the group, originating with the Unibrow. Steam begins to escape from her nose and ears, however I seem to be the only one who notices.

Purple Glasses' demeanor immediately changes. Looking over at the Unibrow she says, "Can you believe she hasn't filled Her water? It has been hours. Mina can't do anything."

I turn back to the Bows, but before I can say anything, Unibrow says to everyone, "Let's play a game." All the girls rise and begin to hop on the cobbled stones of the cold hard basement floor.

As I rise to join them, Unibrow says to me, "You forgot Her water." Then she walks over to the Bows, looks me up and down and announces. "You can see why I'm in charge."

"Don't you understand? She's in charge." The Bows each grab one of Unibrow's hands and they beginning skipping around the room. "She's in charge. She's in charge."

Finally, I break down and sob. I yell at the woman, "Why did you bring me on? Clearly you have someone else who wishes to do the job. Why me?"

It is then that She looks up from her knitting, stares me squarely in the eye and says, "Because you said 'yes,' and agreed to it."

CHAPTER VII

Perspective

Ritual: Creating Boundaries
Element: Air
Planet: Chiron

Boundaries are not just for protection from others, they are also used in keeping ourselves from inflicting harm on others.
At midnight, sit in the center of a dark room. Listen to the night noises, the ticking clocks, the house creaks, the animals stirring. Close your eyes and breathe in this peace. Imagine your inhales and exhales traveling around your body in a clockwise motion. See the air swirl around you and hear it creating a palpable field around you. This field is either a few inches away from your body or a few feet, no more.
Now imagine the breath field traveling around the top of your head to the base of your spine and see the field becoming a sphere. Imagine the sphere pulsing with your energy. Your senses create

the sphere in which you sit. Imagine your core essence emanating
out to this field, strengthening it and clarifying the field.
Bring your awareness back to your breath. Allow your inhales to smooth
out and see the boundary you've created remain static and clear.
Now say the following:
I will bring harm to no one. I am loved and safe. I am protected
always. I will not forsake.

A police officer with a blonde crew cut and cap pulled down low, approaches the driver's side of the black sedan, eying Moa who is sprawled in the back seat with one beefy leg propped up on the center console—cheese-block foot jutting into the front passenger seat, temporarily occupying the large male driver's body.

A second officer with dark hair and aviator sunglasses walks to the passenger side of the car and stands at the ready.

The first officer says curtly, "License and registration, miss."

Hillary hands her license to the officer and digs in the glove compartment, "Um, sorry officer. My friend, Amaranth Najit, needed me to drive for a while. He was…"

"Tired." Moa begins to speak in a low rumbling voice. "I was sooo, sooo, tired. I had to have my friend drive me while I took a nap. Ahhh…Shhhh" She makes a snoring sound for emphasis.

Hillary gives the registration to the officer and with a bemused look, he returns to his squad car to run Hillary's license through the computer.

Moa spies the second officer, still standing next to the passenger side. She leans over and lowers her tinted window, smiles and waves at him. He shakes his head at her in warning.

Then Moa is struck by an idea. "Hillary! I've figured out how to temporarily get Heidi and Molly back in human form." Moa keeps her eyes on the stoic second officer and she continues. "Now it's not permanent, but, it'll do for now."

Turning to the second officer and smiling widely Moa says, "You are a great observer. Have you ever been inhabited before?"

"Sir, I'm going to ask you to be quiet until you are spoken to."

Hillary sees the officer's hand move to rest on his gun holster. "Moa," she whispers, "Please don't talk. Don't you remember what happened in Egypt?"

"As I recall, it all worked out just fine!" Moa gives Hillary a wink. "Trust me."

"Now, officer," Moa continues, leaning her head out of the window, but the officer takes a menacing step forward.

"Sir, I am not going to ask you again. If you don't take this traffic stop seriously, I will arrest you."

Hillary slumps down in the seat, praying that the officer will take pity on her and just give a warning.

But it is not to be. The first officer returns from his cruiser, and proceeds to give a stern lecture. "Do you realize that people have been killed doing what you did? This is punishable with jail time, but I am giving you a ticket and sir, excuse me sir," the officer bangs on the limo's roof to get Moa's attention. She snaps to and he continues. "Whatever your excuse for letting this teenager drive, unless you have been drinking, you should take the wheel. The officer opens up the back door and waits as Moa and Hillary switch places.

"Now drive carefully!"

The officer walks back to his car and the second officer joins him.

"Good Lord!" Hillary shakes with a shudder. "Okay, now take it easy. I'll help you drive.

With the two officers watching, Moa takes the wheel and Hillary gives directions.

"Okay. Put your hands at ten and two. Right pedal is gas, left is brake. The ignition is already on, so all you need to do is put your foot on the brake and shift the car...with that lever there," she points to the gear shift, "and move it to D. Now, take your foot off the brake and gently...gently, Moa... put your foot on the gas. You don't need to press too hard."

Moa slowly shifts into drive. Easing into the road, she inches back into the thick traffic. Then, Hillary lets out a shriek, "Ah!"

"What!" Moa screams too, "What!"

Hillary is waving the ticket the officer just gave her. "$400! I don't have that kind of money!"

"Then you shouldn't have driven on the shoulder," Moa says succinctly. "Many people have been killed by others trying to drive where they shouldn't."

"Well..." Hillary grumbles. "I have no idea how I'm going to pay for this."

"When we get to your place, I'll focus on getting Molly and Heid..." Moa stops, "Uh, oh."

"What is it?" Hillary is panicked.

"I...I've got to pull over." Moa pulls back on to the shoulder and stops. Within seconds of doing this, the body which she currently inhabits jerks and twists, and the head falls back, with mouth gaping open.

"Moa!" Hillary grabs the body's shoulder and shakes with all her might, "Moa. Come back! What about Molly and Heidi?"

70

It is true that I accepted the knitting woman's offer of apprenticeship. The truth punches me right in the gut and, despairing, I collapse onto my cushion.

Surely there is a way to feel better. If the Unibrow doesn't want to work as a team or play, I have no choice but to face her head on in competition.

Watching the girls spinning around me, laughing and playing their made-up games, I am propelled back to my childhood and the boy who tortured me with taunts—another punch in the gut.

On a spring day, the clear air was fragrant with the snap of jasmine and hay and I sat on my father's grave, now grown over with the beautiful, aromatic bushes he so adored. It had been two years since his death and, especially on days like this, I loved to read his books and rest my head against the cool grass alongside his grave marker, a stone obelisk.

The neighbor boy eased off his taunts for exactly one week and then commenced as if the most devastating time of my life had never happened.

I lay, nestled in my favorite spot, imagining that I was snuggled against my father's chest, reading to him as we had done many times before.

On this day, the boy approached me as stealthily as our barn cat and used his words to pounce. "Your father is dead."

"I know." I crunched my body even further into a ball praying that this menace would leave.

"You should die, too. That way, my family can take over this land which they've been trying to do for hundreds of years." He stood over me, breathing hard and loud, obviously upset. "Where you're lying should be my daddy's grave. Now you know what it feels like, only my daddy has no resting place, they burnt him in a fire and he never came home and you should die so he can finally come home, that's what my mom says. She says your family is dirt, dumb dirt, the worst kind of people to inhabit the earth who say because you are Ainu you can squat here on perfectly good land and own it. We are real, civilized Japanese and we have a birthright to this soil..."

He stopped to take a heaving breath and continued, "You and your family have been taking up space here for far too long and we, the real Japanese, are going to take it back." He pulled his leg back as far as he could, aiming at my back and prepared to give me a kick.

"Mina forgot the wa-ter. Mina forgot the wa-ter. The water. The water. Mina forgot the water!" The girls are in front of me chanting, laughing and holding hands in a horrible game of Ring Around the Rosie. Well, I muse, at least I spared myself the memory of the severe beating I incurred.

With a wry smile, I stand up, take each of the Bows' hands and join in, "The water. The water. Mina forgot the wa-ter."

CHAPTER VIII
Long Day

Ritual: Dream Catcher
Element: Tin
Planet: Pluto

*Just before bedtime, fill a glass with water, and as you place the
water next to your bed say:*
*Blessed are my dreams and the messages contained within. I bring
forth my will to send any negative thoughts, experiences, energies
or entities, past, present or future into this glass of water.*
*Trust that your words will be heard. When you awake the next
morning, use the water to hydrate a plant or tree—either indoors
or out. Do not drink the water.*
*As you pour the water into the plant onto the tree imagine
whatever the water has picked up during the night is being
recycled within the earth and will nourish this foliage.*

Amaranth Naiit's head snaps up and the man snorts and smacks his lips as if he's been in a deep, deep sleep. "Hey, where am…who are you?" He gives Hillary a puzzled look. "You're not my scheduled fare!" He rustles around in his pockets and pulls out his wallet, looks at his credit cards and counts his money. "What did you do? Drug me?"

"Um. Didn't you agree to help Moa?" Hillary asks shyly.

"Who's Moa?" The driver says gruffly. "I'm calling the police.

Hillary looks down at the ticket, still in her hand, "Don't worry, I'm sure they're around here somewhere."

The driver picks up his cell phone dials and then says, "Hey, Martha. Who is my fare?" He listens while the dispatch reads the name, then he looks at Hillary in disbelief. "But, I thought George Melotorious was my next pick up. Hause?" He glares at Hillary, leans away from the phone and asks, "Is your name Hillary Hause?" Then he says into the phone, "Never mind, Martha. I guess I've been at it a little too long today. No. No, I'm fine. I'll take Ms. Hause home."

With that, the driver buckles himself into the seat, throws the car into gear and pulls into the now steadily moving stream of cars.

The driver looks straight ahead at the road. "I…uh… Looks like I was mistaken."

"No problem. Do you know where you're going?" Hillary asks kindly.

"8224 Sycamore Lane, Los Tardos. Right?" The driver is now in professional mode.

"Yes," Hillary settles back silently thanking Moa for her magic. "That's the address."

During the car ride home, Hillary tries to figure out what Moa meant about making Molly and Heidi "observers" and rescuing them temporarily. Could she possibly find a way to bring them back to Earth even if they haven't found their own bodies? The traffic is clearing and they manage to make it to her home quickly.

"What do I owe you?" Hillary asks when they pull up in front of her family's small beach bungalow.

"It's on the house." The driver says sheepishly, "I apologize for any inconvenience I caused you.

"It's okay." Hillary smiles kindly. "I hope you're able to get some rest later tonight."

As the sedan pulls away, Hillary drags her bags up to the walkway. Once at the front door, Hillary digs deep into her purse, unearths her keys and opens the deadbolt.

"Hello," she calls, but no one is home.

Grateful for the chance to settle in, she rolls her bags into her first floor cozy, neat bedroom. Gymnastics medals hang on a corkboard and academic awards line a shelf which runs along an entire wall. She is at once comforted and unsettled at being surrounded by her old memories. School was not easy for her, especially high school. A shudder brings back the memory of Krystal Sykes, Darla Melbert and Brenda Stone the "Threatening Three" or "The Threats."

Those days of witchcraft and spells seem so far away. For during her travels, she has learned that beyond the witchcraft, beyond the spells and even beyond the meanness of bullies like "The Threats" we all have the same fears. She walks over to her desk drawer and pulls out a special vial case and opens it. Inside are all her essential oils, neatly arranged in alphabetical order. These oils helped her to cope and perhaps even overcome many of her high school trials.

She also learned that she should never judge someone's behavior, because she may not have the full story. Case in point: Darla Melbert. She taunted Hillary, virtually every day of high school until one day when everything changed.

Hillary picks up a vial of Dragon's Blood oil, unscrews the top and inhales. Instantly, the memory comes.

It was the first day back at school after Thanksgiving vacation. Hillary held the vial tightly as she incanted a protection prayer to herself and planned on anointing Darla's desk when she happened on to a conversation not intended for her ears.

"Did you hear about Darla Melbert?"

"No. What happened?"

Two senior girls, whom Hillary did not know, are at a locker, their heads close.

Hillary backed up behind the corner, out of sight but within earshot.

"Tried to kill herself during the break. I guess her dad was molesting her and her mom didn't believe it."

"How do you know?"

"My sister volunteers at the Mayfield County Hospital and saw the whole thing."

"Oh my God! Is she okay?"

"Well, she's still alive. They kept her in the Psych Ward for a few days then let her go."

"Wow, tough break. Anyway, what are you wearing to Shelby's party Friday?"

Stunned by the news, Hillary walked through the now crowded halls back to her first period class. Hillary slid in to her own desk behind Darla and found it hard to concentrate during the remainder of class.

The bell rang. Hillary followed Darla to her locker and touched her arm.

Darla turned, her eyes stony and said sharply, "What?"

Hillary handed Darla the Dragon oil and said simply, "For protection."

The aroma snaps Hillary back to the present. That was a turning point in Hillary's life. From that moment on, she vowed to right any wrongs to which she bore witness.

However, Hillary realizes that not everyone has had the same insights, and the prospect of encountering—even post-graduation—any of "The Threats" scares Hillary.

The jingle of keys in the front door sends Hillary running to open it. Her mother is dressed in jeans and a brightly colored tunic, and her father wears cargo shorts and a Hawaiian shirt. No doubt, Hillary surmises a gift from her sister, Molly.

"Mom! Dad!"

Hillary is greeted with a chorus of surprised comments and hugs and kisses, which she heartily returns.

"We didn't expect you so soon!" Her mother puts down the groceries in the kitchen and Hillary follows her in.

"Well, I didn't expect to come home, but it was...well, I needed to take care of a few things here."

"Did anything happen between you and Molly?" Her dad's brow is furrowed as he reaches down to tie his tennis shoe.

Laughing to herself, Hillary says, "No, not at all. In fact, we all had a glorious time. But, all things must come to an end eventually."

"Are you hungry?" Her mom pulls out some fresh greens, carrots and crunchy celery. "I was just about to make a salad for lunch."

"Sounds good." Hillary opens the fridge and pulls out a vinaigrette salad dressing and begins to set the table for the three of them.

It is just like old times, the three of them eating together, with no hint of the ugly scene when she'd stormed out of the house after confronting her father about stealing her iPod.

The home phone rings and her dad answers, "Yes. Sure. She's here." He hands the phone to Hillary saying. "Well, good news travels fast. Someone actually knows you're back."

Hillary can't imagine who would know that she was back, when she just found out a few hours ago. Hesitantly, she answers, "Hello."

"Is this Hillary Hause?" The female voice on the other end of the line sounds taut and is faintly familiar.

"Yes," Hillary is still trying to place the voice, "Who is this?"

"It's Krystal Sykes." Now, Hillary places that nasally twang." Can we have lunch?"

"Uh, Krystal, I don't think…"

Before Hillary can finish, Krystal interrupts, "I know we haven't gotten along in the past, but I really need your help."

That seems to be going around, Hillary thinks to herself. First the crone, now Krystal. Who's next, Attila the Hun?

"Well, if you mean by 'haven't gotten along' that you bullied me unmercifully …" Hilary tries to keep her voice steady even though she is increasingly uncomfortable with the thought of Krystal needing her "help." It feels like a trap.

"Please, I beg of you, I can't explain, but you are the only person who can help me." Krystal blurts out, "A terrible hag, an old lady, has been haunting me in my dreams. I haven't slept in three days and I'm going crazy. Believe me, you're the last person I would think of calling, but she keeps saying your name and I don't know why. Hillary, please help me. I think I'm going mad."

"The wa-ter. The wa-ter…" Shame floods through my body as the girls skip around me. Then, suddenly, almost miraculously, I begin to laugh out loud at the absurdity of this game. After all, I think, it is a game. "Mina forgot the wa-ter."

It is the first time, since my father died that I've really enjoyed myself. Funny, I think, that it has to be here. The girls appear to be having fun, too. The knitting woman even taps her toe as she creates loops and knots. The shame I'd felt earlier has been transmuted into joy. Perhaps they are one in the same thing. Then a dark thought jerks me out of my lightness. Why would an Ainu girl be worthy of joy?

Upon this thought, I am kicked from behind. "Ooof!"

It is as if the mean boy from my memory has reached through time and caught my lower rib with his boot. I crumple to the floor wincing with pain and, through my lashes, see the Unibrow smirking at me from across the room.

The Unibrow did this to me, although I have not a clue as to how it happened. I can only lie on the ground, trying to catch my breath. Her eyes bore through me and a twinge of self-doubt begins in the pit of my stomach and grows to engulf my entire lower region. She is evil and, I'm convinced, possesses certain powers beyond my understanding. All I know, is that a terror engulfs my body and I feel compelled to lift my aching body off of the stone floor, limp over to the water basin and get the Unibrow a mug of water!

As I present the mug to the Unibrow, she angles her nose up to the rafters and looks down at me. Her bitter, dark eyes are like two black sesame seeds below her extensive, bristly brow.

Filled with shame, I wander slowly back to my pillow and fall onto it and into a deep, restless sleep.

"Minamo." This was my father's nickname for me, but... "Minamo. Love of my life. Come give me a hug."

My dream is so real, it feels like I'm experiencing it, living, breathing, sensing every glorious moment. A mist covers our field and my father appears above it, hovering over his grave.

"Oh, it is you!" I run to him and hug him, covering him with kisses.

"Of course. Who else would it be?" His eyes crinkle around the edges and his tanned skin is luminous.

"Father. I..." I begin to cry trying to find the words to tell him of my hardships since his passing.

"I already know, Minamo." He places a hand on the top of my head. "Your cleverness can get you into much trouble. Just remember, it can get you out, as well."

"But…I'm all alone!" I sob into his threadbare shirt.

He holds me as the tears pour out, then the words, the story of how mother left me and now I'm here in this godforsaken place. "Please help me," I cry. "Can't you help me?"

"I wish I could, dear Minamo." My father's eyes crackle and sparkle. Suddenly he looks as if he is made of fine crystal with light refracting from all angles. "You chose your current incarnation because your soul has evolved far beyond hand holding. Remember your warrior days? You have a wisdom and heritage beyond your years and it is time to use it."

"But I'm only ten!" I yell. "How, on earth, am I to figure this out? I'm so tired, Father. Can you please give me something, anything that will help?"

"Okay," The darker parts of father's crystal body contrast with the sparkling light and begin to blend with the blue sky. "It will be a long time before you completely understand, however, your mind will be your undoing and your heart will set you free."

"I need my mind to live in everyday life. Have you seen these girls? The Unibrow is cruel, just like the mean boy."

He sighs a weary, ancient sigh.

I continue on, desperate to hold him closer, even for a few seconds, "The Unibrow has special powers. She hurt me and didn't move a muscle. How did she…"

Father cuts me off, "Enough! You are bigger than this, Minamo. You are creating your own prison and you can set yourself free anytime you wish."

Shame floods through me, "I agreed to an apprenticeship. But now I see it is a trap."

He wraps his energy around my entire body and I pull him into every human sense I possess. His warm humor, centered calm, intelligence, joy in life's details, I attempt to capture it all in my body and retain it for later when I might be in need of the nourishing that only he can give.

I awake to the snapping fire, so drained, I can barely lift my head. All the girls are napping on their pillows. A cursory scan reveals that even the knitting woman has settled into slumber. Funny, I think, that she never moves from her chair. The girls and I manage to sleep and even dream.

As I observe the group all curled up on their pillows, I notice something unusual. At rest, each girl has, tucked into her shirt, a glowing jewel. Curious, I lean over one of the Bows to examine hers more closely.

The jewel is perfectly round, grayish green with speckles of yellow deep within. I put my hand on it and see it pulsating deep within her chest. Amazed, I place my hand on her chest and get a jolt of recognition. This is her gift! My hand pulses in rhythm with the gift and a surge of power flows up into my arm and through my entire body. It feels glorious! Shockingly, my hand begins to penetrate her chest and I am able to touch this beautiful gift. Wide eyed, I marvel at the energy and power it gives me.

As I arrive on my pillow, all the girls begin to stir and stretch. Their glowing jewelled gifts are now unlighted, a secret upon waking. I relish my newly acquired knowledge of what they honestly posses. As the fire crackles and pops and I drift in and out of sleep, I wonder if anyone else knows how truly incredible these gifts are and the power they contain.

CHAPTER IX

Bejeweled Servitude

Ritual: Slake the Self
Element: Gold
Planet: Jupiter

Take a walk out in nature or imagine you are doing so. As you take each step, breathe in the vitality of the foliage surrounding you. If you can, take off your shoes and walk in the grass barefoot. As the blades of grass bend under the soles of your feet, imagine the earth pulling out of your body all energy not in alignment with your true self. See it draining toward the center of the earth where it will be recycled and sent to nourish the plants and trees.

Find a large, old tree and place both of your hands upon it. Imagine that it shares its knowledge with you, filling every cell of your body with much needed and desired sustenance and healing.

Ask if the tree has a message, and if it does, listen carefully, for the wisdom you receive now can change your life for the better in a permanent way.

Continue on with your day, knowing that you are completely filled and nourished.

"**H**illary?" Krystal's voice is panicked. "Are you there?"

The sound of Krystal's voice has sucked Hillary back in time. It's almost as if a time tunnel transports her back six years to her middle school hallway as she walks to class after lunch. The feeling is so real she can still smell the sour scent of paper bag lunches and the lingering aroma of cardboard cheese pizza with school district mandated mashed potatoes.

Hillary is twelve and Krystal Sykes, Darla Melbert and Brenda Stone, "The Threats," walk three feet behind her. To a casual observer, they appear to all be walking to class. But, in reality, a slow and steady torture technique has begun and will continue until the final day of high school— the "Style Stalk." No matter how much Hillary sped up or slowed down the group would do the same. If Hillary took another route, they would magically find her and get their verbal jabs in.

On this day, Hillary was feeling nauseated by the hamburger that the kids jokingly dubbed, 'bathmat on a bun." The girls swung in behind her the minute she stepped out of the lunchroom.

"I don't think purple is the right color for some people. Do you girls?" Krystal said in her nasally twang.

A titter of "No's" and "Not at all's" floated forward.

"Especially when they are purple shoes." Krystal chuckled.

Hillary slowed down and stopped at a locker, pretending to look inside her notebook, but the girls were not deterred and they stopped too, leaning against the lockers.

"If I wore purple shoes, I think I'd be humiliated."

"Not if you walked around with ratty, mousy hair." Darla chimed in.

"I wonder if there are actual rats in there?" Brenda giggled, flipping her own silky, long blond hair over her shoulder.

Gales of laughter followed Hillary down the hall, into her classroom and throughout her life.

Those taunts still live within her head and, every so often, when she looks in the mirror while putting on her make-up, the cruelties revisit her.

Krystal, the worst of "The Threats," tortured her throughout middle school and high school. She made virtually every day of Hillary's school-going experience a living hell. And *now* she needs *her* help?!

"Hillary?" The new note in Krystal's voice, the unexpected vulnerability, bring Hillary forward to the present.

"Look, Krystal." Hillary works to control her voice, waves of resentment washing over her. "Whatever your issue, I'm sure you are more than capable of sorting it out without me."

"Can I at least apologize?" The pain in Krystal's voice is palpable.

"Well, that would be refreshing. But why should I accept your apology? It's not like a few words can erase the years and years—I mean days on end, Krystal—of ridicule, name-calling and bullying."

"Okay, okay." Krystal voice cracks as she continues. "I regret doing those things to you. I deserve to rot in hell. Believe me, if I could take them back, I would."

"But you can't." Hillary snaps icily. "The damage has already been done. You didn't just do the bullying yourself, you involved other people and as the years went on the group grew to include my friends. You drew in the people closest to me and then turned them against me."

"I'm so sorry, Hillary." Krystal is crying.

"This is new. Crying for sympathy. I'm having a hard time taking your pleas seriously. There really is nothing you can say. You know what? Let's get this over with. Sure. I accept, Krystal. Now, goodbye." Hillary starts to hang up, but Krystal yells out in desperation. "

I know about Moa." Krystal is sobbing desperately.

Hillary puts the phone back up to her ear. Had she heard correctly? "What did you say?" She lowers her voice to a near whisper.

"I said, I know about Moa." Through her hiccupping sobs, Krystal continues, "In my last dream, a girl named Moa said she would guide me to safety, and she told me to call you today."

A pang of jealousy hits Hillary in the ribs. "You actually think Moa could be your guide. She is an incredible…amazing…spirit. You, on the other hand are…well, I am having a hard time choosing the right word. Obnoxious? Terrible? Despicable? You taunted me every single school day. Do you know the harm you caused?"

Hillary lets silence sit between them, listening to Krystal's sniffling, her own eyes smarting with anger.

After a moment, Hillary says in a tight voice, "Can you give me one reason why I would ever – EVER – raise a finger to help you?"

"Because you are better than me." Krystal's speaks so softly, Hillary almost cannot hear the words.

She is too shocked to speak and Krystal continues. "Remember on the first day of middle school, I asked you to eat lunch and you said "No?" Hillary digs into her memory but cannot remember such an incident. Krystal continues, "You didn't even look at me and when I asked, you brushed me off." Krystal's voice is even and calm now.

A faint memory forms in Hillary's mind. The first day of school was a blur. She was terrified that she wouldn't belong, might miss a class, would forget the combination to her locker. She can't even place Krystal back then. Hillary's only guess is that she was so overwhelmed, she didn't have room to even acknowledge another person.

"All the things you did to me, day in and day out, was because of one interaction on the first day of school?" Hillary is astonished.

"I'm sorry." Krystal begins to weep softly and Hillary sits in silent disbelief. "These dreams…they've been wearing me down, Hillary. I'm exhausted. I don't know who Moa is, but it was my only hope to stop the crone's terrible visitations. Please, please. Can't we meet? I don't know why, but I know that if we can get together everything will be better."

"Better for who?" Hillary asks wryly.

"For both of us."

"Well, I guess we'll see about that," Hillary says. "I'll meet you at Demo's Café in fifteen minutes."

As she hangs up and changes clothes, readying herself to meet Krystal, she gets a pang about Moa. Why did she abandon the driver's body? And why on earth had her spirit friend contacted the leader of "The Threats" and her arch nemesis, Krystal Sykes? And why did Krystal need to meet her in person?

The café is almost empty after the lunch rush and Hillary sees Krystal, her back to the entrance, already seated at a small table, which is tucked away in a corner.

Hillary orders an iced mocha from the counter and approaches the table.

"Krystal?"

When the girl hears her voice, Krystal rises and rushes toward Hillary.

"Oh, Hil." Krystal holds on for dear life and then looks deeply into her eyes.

Shocked by this unusual display, Hillary backs away.

"Hil. It's me, Molly."

"Mol…" Hillary is beyond words and gapes at Krystal as she collapses into her seat.

"It's me. Moa visited Krystal and hounded her until she gave in and called you. Then, she transported my *Ka* energy body into Krystal."

"Okay. If you're Krystal, then where's Heidi?" Hillary can't quite wrap her brain around seeing her sister in such an incongruous "location."

"I don't know." Molly squirms in her seat as she has not yet gotten completely comfortable with her new state. "One thing I do know is that we don't have much time."

During the day, I sit quietly, acquiescing to the Unibrow's whims—I have now resigned myself to her tyrannical rules—my job, she proclaims, is to watch the woman knitting—who does nothing, says nothing—and I bide my time until rest time.

Ah, the time when everyone slumbers and I can sneak about, examining, testing and yes, savoring the tremendous jolt of strength and power contained within each girl's personal gift. The power I gain from touching these beautiful jewels only lasts for a minute within me and then dissipates quickly. Until, that is, I come to the Unibrow. Her gift is quite small and barely glows. In fact, it barely pulsates at all, but limps along in a sluggish, *tink, tink, plunk, plunk.*

I rush to my pillow just as she awakes.

The days of servitude go faster as I anticipate what I may discover as I perform my rest time experiments, deftly crawling from one subject to the next, learning about each girl's deepest gift and gathering and storing the energy in my own body. Then one evening, I decided to press my hand to every girl in the circle, as they sleep. What I find astonishes me. An escape plan floods my brain. A door, which had been previously hidden to me, now appears clear as day! It is directly behind the water basin, from which I've filled hundreds of mugs full of water for knitting woman and "her highness the Unibrow." How could I have missed it? Perhaps, I reason, I have been too weak, up until now, to devise a plan to relieve myself of this horrid place.

Here is my plan: I will wait until everyone is asleep, including the knitting woman, and after filling myself by placing my hand on each girl's gift, I will wrench open the door and flee into the night. After that, who cares! I'm filled with power and by using all the girls' gifts, including the knitting woman—whose jewel is even dimmer than the Unibrow—I'll use their combined powers and my wits, my luscious brain to get me out of any trouble.

I spend the morning before my escape sweeping the stone hearth, straightening and fluffing the pillows and, of course, providing water for the Unibrow and knitting woman. Rest time cannot come soon enough.

Come rest time, however, no one seems in the mood to lie down and sleep. One of the Bows looks at me, her head resting on her pillow, eyes at half-mast, and says, "You're great to put up with all of this, Mina. I could never do it."

I almost feel sorry for her, for all of them. But then, I catch sight of the Unibrow and she narrows her eyes, a hairy scowl of a warning, and I know that I am resolved to leave here forever.

When everyone is asleep, I make my way around the group, pressing my palm, pulling the energy into my body. Finally, I make my way to the Unibrow's sleeping body. She snores loudly as I put my hand on her chest, the little *tink, tink, plunk plunk* of a jewel barely filling a fingernail's worth of my energy. Then I think, I wish I could take a jewel with me. Wouldn't that be nice? I say to myself. The Unibrow answers me with a sleepy, "Yes." And as she drifts deeper into slumber, her jewel gift adheres to my hand.

Panicked, I pluck my hand—with the dim jewel attached—out of her chest. Frightened by this gruesome new discovery, I attempt to flick it off like a scrap of flypaper to no avail. Shocked and appalled that a fleeting wish could actually come true, I plunge my hand back and try to return the gift to its original home, but it will no longer stay. It's as if the Unibrow's agreement willed her jeweled gift to me, whether I wanted it or not.

The Unibrow slightly awakens and I run past the water basin and use my supercharged body to pry open the heavy, wooden door and slip up the stairway into the damp, cold night. Fearing pursuit, I continue to run through the streets until I come to a forest. The grove of trees is my cover as I dodge in an out of them, moving deeper into the forest. As I slow my pace, the moon becomes less and less visible through the dense foliage. Enormous trees blot out any light that might have gotten through from above. Sitting on a patch of soft moss and using a tree trunk as a back support, I calm myself. The darkness seems to drain the remainder of my pilfered jewel energy reserve.

For the first time in a very long while, I am able to sleep and I awake in the forest, the moss tickling my back, in total darkness. How long have I slept? Perhaps I'm in a world of perpetual night? Although awake, I am exhausted. It is as if every ounce of energy has been drained from my body.

I had not noticed before because of the distraction with the Unibrow, however, I now find myself suddenly in dire need of sustenance. The food given to me by the warmth of the fire was bread and water, hardly a feast. Although we were given meager crumbs while I was in the small enclave of girls, I'm confused by why those morsels did nothing to satisfy my rumbling stomach. Even water seemed to have no effect on quenching my thirst. A wave of fear passes through my body as I run my tongue over my parched lips.

My escape seems to have sapped me of every last ounce of energy. Drifting in and out of consciousness, it becomes evident that I will soon die and I prepare to do so. In a dream state, I recall the Unibrow's dim jewel and I awaken to find it stuffed under the folds of my shirt.

Even though the jewel is dim, it catches a small bit of starlight, which peeks in through the canopy of trees. I hold it up and look at it carefully. The iridescent, blue green octahedron catches bits of starlight on its beveled angles.

"The beginning of the end," I think as I ingest the jewel gift by pressing it into my own chest and inhaling. Unsure of what will happen, I close my eyes and wait for the results. Not knowing how long the effects will stick with me, I dare not imagine how long it will be before or if I might need more nourishment.

Crying softly, I realize this is the end of the beginning. I have consumed the gift and I know in time it, in turn, will consume me.

CHAPTER X

Containers

Ritual: Blessing the Water
Element: Platinum
Planet: Moon

---

*Fill a glass of water and find a comfortable quiet place to sit.
Breathe deeply, holding the water with both hands.*

*Now, imagine that you can send any thought or vibration
into the water and change or enhance its properties for
your healing benefit. It is possible to do this, however, your
commitment and intention is the most important element in
this ritual.*

*Close your eyes and imagine the word "Love" spelled out in front
of you. What do the letters look like? Does the word have a sound?
A taste? A scent?*

Say the word aloud. As you say it, imagine that the word moves from your throat, to your heart and out through your hands into the water you are holding. Continue to say the word, "Love." With every repetition, see love transforming the water into a healing elixir. When you are finished, drink the water. Imagine that the love is flowing to every cell in your body, nourishing, feeding and filling your aura with the love you've just created.

"Moa took over a driver's body earlier today, Mol. I think you're right about not having much time. Not only do we need to find Heidi, but we also need to find your own bodies." Hillary is still shocked to be talking with her sister who has temporarily taken up residence in the body of Krystal Sykes, her arch enemy from high school.

Not completely convinced, Hillary searches Krystal's visage for any semblance of her sister, but is unable to find one. The words her nemesis says are certainly unlike anything she would normally say, but she is still hesitant to believe that her sister is using Krystal's body as a "container."

As Hillary watches, a spark of recognition ignites. Molly has always been meticulous about her food and drink. Hillary remembers a time when Molly wiped off every single utensil as she prepared her coffee. Now Hillary watches as Krystal receives her coffee from the server and carefully shakes in a half packet of sugar and puts in a splash of cream. The clincher for Hillary identifying her sister's true identity is when she takes the stirring straw, swirls it around three times, taps it on the edge of the mug and then gently uses it to sample the drink. Hillary has watched this exact ritual during virtually every breakfast they had together.

"Mol!" Hillary gasps, "It really is you." The sisters begin to laugh uproariously.

When they finally settle, Hillary takes a sip of her mocha and leans in, "Okay, here's what I think we should do. If Moa put you in Krystal, Heidi can't be to far behind. I'm not sure how much time we have, but I think we should increase our odds of finding her and split up."

"I don't!" Molly says. "Who knows how long I have in this current body. I'd hate to suddenly get back to wherever I was before and lose contact with you."

"Okay." Hillary smiles. "You're right. Well, where do you think Heidi is? Should we go back home?"

"Why don't we break out the 'gifts' we have?" Molly smiles. "I'll tell you what I sense and you tell me what you see."

Hillary closes her eyes and shakes her head. "All I see is purple. Purple ceiling or sky, purple people, purple ground. Not sure what this means."

"Let's see." Molly puts her hand on her sister's. "Okay. I sense that she's somehow closed off. It's not bad or uncomfortable, but she's alone and closed off."

The sisters look at each other for a moment then burst out laughing.

"So Heidi is either a dressed as a grape standing in the middle of nowhere or swimming by herself in a pool of grape Jell-o."

"Wherever she is, I think we should get going. Anything is better than sitting here and talking about it." Hillary gets up.

"Wait!" Molly grabs her arm. "Look out there."

Both women look through the large plate glass window, across the street to see a carnival set up in a small lot. Several clowns are playing around and juggling balls, and a man on purple stilts paces back and forth with long awkward strides.

Hillary shrugs, "That looks like as good a place to start as anywhere else."

The two dash across the street, but before they can go in, they are stopped by a security guard who babbles and gurgles at them and points to the ticket kiosk.

"But we only want to see one thing, then we'll be right back," Molly pleads.

"Gringle di booga." The husky security officer looks a little wobbly on his feet as he blocks the entrance.

"Obviously some drugs are in play…" Fuming, Molly says as she walks toward a small wooden ticket kiosk at the front of the lot. In it sits a lanky teenage girl with spikey hair dyed pink, wearing a tie-dye t-shirt and thumbing through a magazine.

"Yeah." The girl looks at Molly through her heart shaped sunglasses with lavender lenses.

"Two tickets please," Molly says anxiously as she digs in her purse.

Shoving the sunglasses on the top of her head, the girl reveals a mischievous twinkle in her eye. "Sorry. We're all out."

"No attitude, young lady." Molly snaps at the insolent teen.

"Mol," Hillary says, putting a hand on her sister's shoulder.

"Okay, but you don't need a ticket." The teen goes back to her magazine.

"Hey," Molly yells angrily, "I need a ticket. My daughter is in there somewhere and I need one now."

"Look, you don't need a ticket." She smiles, then adds, "Mommy."

For a moment, neither Hillary nor Molly knows how to react, then the girl hops off her stool and exits the booth to smother her mother with kisses and hugs.

"Oh, Mommy," Heidi says. "I missed you so much!"

"How did you know it was me?" Molly is near tears.

"I guessed." Heidi laughs. "Aunt Hillary gave you away!" She twirls around and gives her mother another big squeeze.

"Just a minute," Heidi motions to two teens working at the concession stand. One of them slides into the ticket booth and Heidi says, "I didn't want the booth to go unattended. Where to?"

"We've got to find Adem and then get you all back to your real bodies," Hillary says. "When Moa was inhabiting her last body, she suddenly had to leave."

"My guess is because the driver wanted his body back." Molly adds, "I can't imagine where Adem is or even if he's here."

"If we found each other, we'll find him. How does it feel in there, you two?" Hillary eyes her sister and niece. "I mean, is it cramped or stuffy? Do you feel the other person's feelings or hear their thoughts?"

"No, but it does feel a bit like being in a hotel room," Molly says. "It's comfortable, but not quite home."

"Speaking of…" Hillary escorts her sister and niece down the sidewalk, away from the carnival's entrance.

"I kind of like this body." Heidi looks down at her developing shape. "My legs are kind of achy, though."

"It's not at all the package I imagined for you," Molly says. "But it does give me a frightening glimpse into the future."

"I know!" says Hillary. "I mean, imagine Adem as a full grown male!"

"Oh!" Molly turns and looks at Hillary. "You are brilliant!" She hugs her confused sister and abruptly heads back to the carnival. "I just realized where Adem is. Come on!"

Molly makes her way through a crowd that has formed at the fair's entrance and approaches the stoic security guard.

"Hello." Molly looks deep into the guard's eyes and takes a couple of sniffs.

He returns her words with a huge grin and he says, "DA!"

Carefully Molly looks around then whispers, "Adem? Love, is that you in there?"

The guard wobbles his head and throws his arms around Molly, engulfing her in a tremendous bear hug. "Goo. Gee. Bah!"

Molly takes the guards hand and leads him away from the entrance, as Hillary says hesitantly, "What if it's not Adem?"

Molly peers at his face. "His pupils indicate no drugs. No alcohol on his breath and it is a pretty odd coincidence that Adem was so close to Heidi…"

"And that this grown man is babbling like a baby," Heidi adds.

"A mother is supposed to know these things I'll give you that," Hillary says warily. "I guess the best place to go now is home." She pauses to check out Adem as he holds Molly's hand tightly and wobbles down the sidewalk, his legs looking unsteady.

"When we get home, we can figure out our plan of attack," Hillary suggests. "Mom and Dad are going to be quite surprised!"

"Should we tell them?" Heidi asks.

"Not right away." Hillary says, "It may be a little to hard to imagine that their oldest daughter and niece and grandson are housed in other people's bodies and that they have temporarily lost their own."

Once they are back at home, Hillary, Molly and Heidi make a beeline for Hillary's bedroom.

Shutting the door, Hillary takes a seat on her bed. "I think we should start with using our gifts. That worked for Mol and I to find you, Heidi. I'll have to admit, I was skeptical at first, that purple reference…"

"I know." Mol settles onto an overstuffed chair with Heidi. "Okay, Hillary what do you see?"

98

"The back of someone's head. Brown hair. Curly and thick."

"Male or female?" Molly pats Adem's head. He has curled up in the fetal position next to Molly's chair, has fallen asleep, sucking his thumb and is snoring loudly.

"Male." Hillary sighs. "I don't see anyone's face. It's very frustrating. I can't move around, just observe, so I'll say more about the surroundings. Blue fabric, gray walls. A cubicle. Actually, a sea of cubicles. Mol, I think you're working in an office building. Heidi, what do you hear?"

"No one is speaking, but I can hear the sound of people typing on the computer. Wait! I do hear someone speaking on the phone. It's not in English…"

"Is it Japanese?" Molly asks.

"I don't know what that sounds like," Heidi says.

"Well, what I sense is that there is a lot of tension around one person."

"Are you focusing in on your body or Heidi's? Hillary asks.

"Both."

"But what if they're not together."

"I think they are…"

"But what if they're not…" Hillary stands up, "I think you're doing it wrong, Molly. You should focus on each body separately."

"I didn't tell you how to see things, don't tell me how to feel."

Suddenly Heidi interrupts their bickering. "I hear English!" she yells.

"Where?" Hillary sits back down. "What are they say…"

"Shhhh…" Molly puts her hand on Hillary's leg then whispers, "Let her listen!"

Heidi sways a little back and forth, then closes her eyes.

"It's music! I hear "The Star Spangled Banner." Now, an announcer is talking about baseball," Heidi says.

"Keep going, sweetie." Molly strokes Heidi's arm.

"Now a phone is ringing and a woman talks about Chance In Bora Bora. She just keeps repeating that when the phone rings."

"Let's see what we have. An office full of cubicles, a male with brown curly hair, "The Star Spangled Banner" and a Chance in Bora Bora." Hillary chuckles. "Oh, yeah. This'll be a piece of cake."

Within seconds of consuming Unibrow's jewel, I am restored. Much to my surprise, I feel sated and my regret for consuming the jewel and its potential costly effects on me wane. Perhaps this is payback for the torture the Unibrow put me through. My energy now fully restored, I am able to continue on my journey through the woods to whatever may await me beyond this dark patch of woods.

However, another thing happens as I begin to make my way through the forest. My limbs, although rejuvenated, feel odd, leaden and thick. Since I cannot see clearly, I must wait to emerge from the darkness to examine my body. At present, I step over rocks, carefully sidestep fallen trees and crunch through blankets of leaves, not knowing exactly in which direction to head but certain that I am moving away from my previous location of imprisonment by the knitting woman. As I meander along, it occurs to me that I don't feel quite like myself.

The explanation playing inside my head is something like this: If matter consists of cells, atoms, molecules, and each has a definitive boundary which humans have come to know as "real," then it feels like my body has evolved beyond that, beyond the perception of those who "see" the vibrations of others.

In other words, I feel like…nothing.

Wait. I stop for a moment. Did I just say to myself that I am nothing? I chuckle to myself as I step over stones and snap twigs in my path toward the light. Perhaps I'll ask someone, when I find them, for a mirror. Better yet, I can find out if anyone sees or hears me.

In the distance, I can just make out shimmering light. This self talk, I reason, is just an exercise to keep me from feeling bad about taking the Unibrow's gift. Even thinking about the event does not seem to bother me as much as it had at first. I have, at least for the time being, become fearless—no doubt a side effect of consuming the gift.

It isn't until I come out of the woods that I realize there is daylight. Apparently, the trees in the forest masked the sun so well, that it isn't until the forest opens up into a clearing that I am able to feel sun on my skin for the first time in what seemed a very long time. How wonderful! I close my eyes and lay on a patch of warm grass soaking up the radiant light.

A low rumbling begins in my belly and, suddenly, I feel queasy. Assuming that this is a side effect from consuming the jewel, I squirm around with eyes still shut until a loud belch escapes from my mouth. Perhaps some food and water will settle my stomach. The sun rakes across my eyes as I open them and rise. But I stop short when I see my feet. Toes with wiry hairs protruding from each joint extend out from thin bony feet. Veined, wrinkled legs extend up from each jutting ankle bone. I jump when I see my hands, which match the legs, except for my right forearm which is swollen and red.

Frightened for my life, I run as fast as I can, imagining that I can somehow escape that which I have come to embody. I stare in disbelief at my arms and legs, running in terror in all directions, running from myself. Finally, I find a small group of huts outside of which several children are kicking a small ball around in the dirt.

"Hello!" A little girl looks up and runs toward me. "Want to play?"

Surprised at the friendly greeting, I freeze.

"You seem shy. It's okay, I'm shy, too." She grabs my hand and much to my shock, it is back to its normal state.

"Thank you." I am surprised by the sound of my normal voice.

Grateful to have someone so kind to play with, I shake off my disturbing experience as a bad dream.

CHAPTER XI

A Chance in Bora Bora

Ritual: Expansion
Element: Silver
Planet: Earth

Lower vibrational emotions like anger and fear cause our auras to contract. This contracted state of existence is draining on every part of your body, mind and spirit. The contracted state is meant to protect you from any attacks however, if your aura remains contracted, you can get sick and it is harder to heal.

By expanding your aura, you relax the parts of yourself, which attract positive events, people and feelings. You also increase your ability to heal yourself while in an expanded state.

Find a quiet place where you will remain undisturbed. Sit or lie down and begin with three breaths. On the last exhale open your mouth wide and let your breath out loudly with a "Haaaa!"

If you wish, you may make sounds as you exhale. Now, bring your awareness to your neck. Breathe three more times using the open mouth exhale and see the back of your neck opening up. See an opening the size of a quarter appear which will allow any tension or negativity to run out of your body. Imagine that through this opening, negative thoughts, feelings, other people's thoughts or energy, fall to the ground (away from your body) where it will be reabsorbed by Source.

Finally, send a relaxed, healthy, positive feeling into the opening at the back of your neck and imagine that the feeling grows big enough to surround your body with a feeling of protection and love. Now, send that feeling out as far as you feel comfortable— some people will feel comfortable with a few inches of expansion and others will expand over a few miles.

Continue to breathe normally and know you are surrounded by love and protection in your expanded state. Drink plenty of water after you are finished.

Know that in this state, you attract what you put out into the world. So, it is advisable to watch what happens for the following 24 hours. If you keep your thoughts positive, you may find that you attract positive events or people to you.

"A Chance in Bora Bora," says Molly, stroking the sleeping security guard's hair, or more precisely, Adem's curly hair. "Maybe it is a company giving away a chance to win a trip to Bora Bora, Tahiti?"

Hillary marvels at the odd collection before her in her room. Molly is in the body of Krystal Sykes, Heidi's energetic body is housed in a lanky teenage girl with pink spikey hair and Adem's is within a husky security guard's body loudly snoring at the foot of Molly's chair.

As unusual as this setup is, each of them must find her own physical body before these people decide they want them back.

"Let's do a search for companies giving away trips to Tahiti." Hillary says, "It's a start."

She sits at her desk and turns on her computer—a gift from her parents for passing honors English last year in school—and waits. "There are a million ways to interpret the information we each received. It could take longer than we have to check out all our leads."

"Look how we found Heidi and Adem," Molly says. "You have to keep an open mind, Hil."

Hillary types in the information and reads the results, "Cherry-O Soda is giving away a trip to Switzerland. Champra Cosmetics has a trip to Italy and Chorcom Inc. has an annual giveaway to Hawaii."

"What if you searched for exactly what Heidi said," Molly interjects.

Hillary types in "blue office cubicles, a male with brown curly hair, "The Star Spangled Banner" and a Chance in Bora Bora."

"Nothing of significance."

"Didn't the old book say that our bodies were in Japan?" Molly suggests, "Why not add that to our search."

Hillary does and carefully searches each link for clues. None of them yield anything of significance.

"Did you search everything, Hil?" Molly asks with a tinge of judgment.

"Yes, " Hillary reacts defensively, "Of course, I searched everything." She mocks her sister's tone on the last few words.

"Are you sure?" Molly rises and stands behind Hillary.

"I searched everything I can search." Hillary leans away from the monitor. "See for yourself."

"What about this one?" Molly points to an unchecked search result.

"That's in Japanese," Hillary says dryly.

"I see that, but it can't hurt," Molly prods.

"Fine. You go ahead." Hillary stands up in a huff and motions for Molly to sit. "If you think you can do it then go ahead." She crosses her arms over her chest and watches as Molly clicks on, then peruses, the site.

After a full minute of silence, Hillary says smugly, "Well?"

Molly throws her hands up in defeat, "I can't read any of it. No English whatsoever."

"See?" Hillary nods her head in satisfaction.

Molly stands and confronts Hillary, "What's that supposed to mean?"

"Just what I said. You can now see that no one can read that website. It is impossible."

As the sister's argue, Heidi slips quietly into the seat and begins to work, then, as her aunt and mother's argument has reached its peak she announces, "Got it!"

Stunned, both women gape at the girl.

Heidi continues, "The name is Chansynburabura Corporation established in 1983 by the Togakashi brothers. It's based in Kamakura, Japan." Smiling she looks up at the woman. Then she continues, "I found this picture in the 'Careers' section."

They all gasp. Except for Adem who gives a loud snort in his sleep. The picture shows a large room which houses a hundred or more cubicles with blue fabric walls. "Here's the best part, Heidi clicks on another image and reads, "The Chansynburabura Corporation recently acquired the American company, Manterson Group. Manterson recently closed its corporate headquarters in Hawaii as well as the satellite offices in Egypt and relocated all employees to Kamakura, Japan."

"That's pretty amazing." Molly is still agape.

"You would say that." Hillary gives Molly a snide look.

"Well, I wasn't the first to be visited by Moa in Hawaii and I didn't jump on a plane with Moa to Egypt to find the statue of Ku, but it seems to me we might have a shot at finding our bodies if we pool our resources." Molly glares at Hillary.

"You certainly act like an expert." Hillary glares back.

"Come on, people!" Heidi has had enough. "We don't have a lot of time. Let's not spend it fighting."

"She's right." Hillary looks at Molly. "Sorry." Then, Hillary looks at her niece, "Google Translate?"

Heidi gives a proud nod then says authoritatively, "We're all under a lot of tension. My question is how, on earth do we get to Japan?"

"Well, last time we went to Japan, the opportunity just showed up," Heidi says whimsically. "What if we went to the airport to catch a ride?"

"That is absolutely preposterous!" Molly cries. "Let's do it!"

"I'm Selerani." The sweet girl who has invited me to play gives my hand a quick squeeze and I am immediately at ease. "Call me Seli."

She leads me into a circle of children ranging from about four years to twelve years old. I watch them watching me. Seli deftly passes the ball to an older boy with scruffy brown hair, as she introduces me around, "This is Mina. She's shy."

The older boy kicks the ball to me and I side kick it to a little girl whose sad eyes peek through her long bangs. I've played this game before, and soon they're shouting, "Go Mina!" as I kick the ball toward a line of branches meant to be a goal.

Cheers all around as I score!

The children's faces become snowy and my legs become wobbly as I fall face first into the leafy branches of the goal.

I awaken to a woman's voice in a one-sided conversation, "She's here. No she's not one of us but she still deserves to be comfortable in her journey."

Though my vision is blurred, I can feel the comfort of a soft hay bed underneath my body and a cool cloth on my forehead.

My mouth is dry despite the kind woman's efforts to squeeze water into it. I think, "Where am I?"

"You are safe, dear." The woman's lips do not move as she speaks and it dawns on me that she is speaking to me telepathically. "I'm speaking with you through thought wave patterns, Mina. Thoughts are quite powerful, and our tribe has found that telepathy is the most efficient way to communicate. We tried to give you mashed fruit, but it seems that you cannot keep food down. It seems that your body is rejecting all forms of nourishment. You must find something on which to subsist or you will perish."

She puts her hand on my head and I instantly feel calm. She brings her other hand up into a sweeping motion over her head and I catch a glimpse of a light emanating from her chest. Her jewel gift is visible and she is awake!

"Yes." She answers my thought. "Healers have cultivated their gifts, and this awareness makes the jewel inside their heart space stronger and thus more visible."

A wave of shame engulfs my body as I remember retrieving, then consuming, the Unibrow's gift. I wonder how she has fared without her precious jewel.

"You did what you needed to do in difficult circumstances, Mina." The woman rises to leave, but not before adding, "Unfortunately I cannot aid you further in finding sustenance. We did our best to feed you with our unique type of nourishment, however, your acceptance and assimilation of food is solely up to you. I pray, for your sake, you will find a more humane way of sustaining your life in future." She opens the fabric flap of the hut and exits.

I am left alone with utterly no idea of how to live. The longer I wait, the more dire my needs will be and that knowledge sends a shiver through my weary body.

Where is my guidance? I cry bitterly for my father, but he does not come. Since food no longer offers me life-sustaining properties, I must find another way to feed myself. Surely there is an alternative to choosing between death or stealing and consuming unsuspecting people's jewel gifts.

Fear bursts from my belly into my diaphragm creating a fist-sized knot. Death takes on an entirely different meaning and this knot has a voice. The fear knot shoves itself against my organs, pressing out my breath. I can barely inhale as I hear the knot say, "Your mind is only a small, insignificant part of the equation. It is your DNA which must continue on, it is your birthright to survive, to live and yes, to thrive. You can only accomplish this by taking what will be of little use to another or most likely, will never be used at all. No one will perish. In fact, a human's life is strengthened by adversity. You will be joining a part of a divine ecosystem of learning. You've been wondering why you are here, for what purpose you were born onto this Earth. Here is the answer: You must live, preserve the divine body, which you possess so that you may perpetuate a human's greatest learning. As a celestial teacher, you will roam the Earth, providing first hand teaching to those who need to acquire soul enhancing knowledge with regards to their gifts. Not only is this your duty," the pressure intensifies so much that I can take only a hiccup of an inhale, "this, Mina, is your destiny."

Before my mind has a chance for rebuttal, I am out of bed with a strength beyond my comprehension and I am propelled outside, into the now dark courtyard of the little community of huts. Instantly, I find myself at the foot of the littlest girl's pad. She sleeps soundly, her bangs nearly cover her eyes and, except for the rise and fall of her chest, does not move.

Her beautiful jewel glows beneath her shirt, nestled unsuspecting, an innocent available for the taking.

My heart pounds as I crouch down, careful not to disturb her parents who are sprawled, snoring across the hut.

"Are you crazy?!" My mind manages a quick jab of a thought before my body chimes in. "This child has yet to realize her true gifts. Some humans never use them in a lifetime, nor many lifetimes. Such a waste."

My hand is ready, my arm is cocked like a bow and arrow, then, once more, my mind slips in a caveat, "Remember how the Unibrow said, 'yes?' You must procure an agreement from this girl—a verbal contact of sorts.

"How on earth can I do this, I'd rather die," My mind is in a moral battle with the slippery thoughts of my body, desperate to keep me from taking this poor child's gifts for nourishment.

"Death will not cure destiny, Mina." My hand gently presses to the girl's tiny ribcage, submerges briefly. It is only then that I make my mental request of her. "May I please have this jewel? I am weak and need sustenance."

Her little mouth curls in a smile as she breathes a wispy, "Yes."

With deft precision, I extract her jewel and gobble it down, savoring the light, the power, the life fulfilling properties contained within the glowing goodness and I slip noiselessly out of the hut, back into the woods, promising myself, "This is the last time."

CHAPTER XII
Slippery Secret

Ritual: Frenemy Release
Element: Copper
Planet: Mars

At 11:30pm on any day of the week,
sit in a quiet space where you will remain undisturbed for at least
one half hour.
Picture your Frenemy in front of you. See them as clearly as
possible in your mind's eye. Now, say the following to them:
I invoke grace and peace, love and light, together all we will
share is right.
Imagine a blue light appears from the heavens and surrounds you
both with an incredible sense of wellbeing. Then say:
Release the past. Release the pain. What was wrong within me,
make right again.

Imagine that the blue light dissolves the current picture you created of your Frenemy. Know that you have dissolved the negative within you and that, through thought and deed, you can manifest friendship and love with this person and any other person you wish.

Grabbing the keys to her car, Hillary calls to her parents who are reading in the living room, "I'm heading out with some friends. Don't wait up."

"Wait a minute!" Her mother rushes into the hallway but stops in her tracks when she sees the motley crew in front of her. "First of all you just got here. Second, and this is more important, who are these people?"

"Um, this is Krystal Sykes." Hillary's mother raises her eyebrows upon hearing the name.

"Well, I've heard your name enough. But last time I saw you, you were about eight years old. What brings you back after all these years?" Mrs. Hause eyes Krystal suspiciously.

"I wanted to apologize to Hillary." Molly does her best to look apologetic but with Krystal's face, the expression appears more stern than intended.

Hillary continues the introductions, motioning to the pink-haired teen. "This is...Sally...Shore."

"Nice to meet you, Mrs. Hause." Heidi tries to sound dignified.

"Please, call me Ruby." Mrs. Hause relaxes a bit and gives a slight smile to the guests.

Hillary continues on to the husky security officer, now groggily towering above them all, "And this is Mike Rengler. He works with Sally at the carnival."

"Why do you need to go to the airport in such a hurry?" Hillary's mom eyes Adem's looming figure suspiciously.

"Oh," Hillary adds. "Well, we need to pick up some friends of Mike's."

Ruby leans in and sniffs Adem's breath then looks him up and down. "You know what? I'll go with you. We haven't had enough time to get acquainted."

"But Mom..." Hillary protests.

"Just let me grab my hat and we'll be off!" Ruby goes back to the bedroom to retrieve her hat.

While she is gone, Molly whispers, "We can't let her come. How are we going to explain this to her?" Then, she sniffs the air and looks stricken. "Mike! I think we should all try to go to the restroom before we go. She shoves Mike into the bathroom and closes the door."

When Ruby returns, she has a brightly colored floppy hat and tortoise shell sunglasses. "Let's go!" she declares, romping out to the car.

As Molly exits the restroom with a contented Adem, she whispers to Hillary, "That was interesting..."

All five people squeeze into Hillary's small SUV and the trip starts off in silence. Before Hillary leaves the driveway, Adem is fast asleep, snoring away and leaning on Ruby's shoulder—a line of drool travels its way down his stubbled cheek to his chin.

"This is a unique one. Where ever did you find him?" Ruby does her best to get comfortable under Mike's crushing weight.

"We, uh..." Hillary exchanges looks with Molly. "Okay, mom. I'm not sure how to explain this to you, but Krystal here is really Molly and Sally is Heidi and Mike is baby Adem. It may be hard to believe, but, well they've lost their bodies and we are on our way to Japan to retrieve them."

Molly helps out, "We're not really sure how we're going to get there. It sounds quite silly as I say it and I'm sure you've noticed that it's unlike me to not plan ahead but we only have a limited amount of time. And…and…" unable to go on she settles into an uneasy silence.

No one speaks for what seems like an eternity until Ruby chortles. Then she snorts, then she guffaws. She slaps her leg, laughing so hard that it catches on. Soon Heidi grabs her belly and cracks up and Molly begins to giggle. Seeing the ridiculousness of their situation, Hillary begins to laugh, too. The entire group falls into wave upon wave of laughter. When one person stops another keeps it going. Then just when it dies down, another begins again.

Finally, between giggles Heidi asks, "So what do you think, Grandma?"

"Grandma! Ha! Grandma! Ha! HA!" Ruby begins to laugh and the whole car stares.

Hillary looks at her mother with concern, guessing she might have been pushed too far. "Maybe we've given her too much information all at once, and her brain just snapped," she whispers to the others.

But when Ruby catches her breath, she smiles gently and says, "I'm not Grandma. It's me, Moa!"

Hillary slams on the brakes and pulls into the nearest parking lot, a stretch of asphalt at a minimart. Then she turns around in her seat to look at Moa directly. "Are you kidding me? Moa, you just about gave me a heart attack. You can't just …Oh, give me a hug!"

After a substantial greeting, Moa says, "Okay. Hillary. We have a plane waiting to take us to Japan."

"From John Wayne airport?" Molly asks.

"Sure. Why not?" Moa chuckles. "Remember, you're in rented bodies and we need to get you all to Kamakura in one piece as quickly as possible."

"Onward!" Hillary calls as she turns in to the Departure parking lot at John Wayne Airport in Orange County, California. "Let's hope no one needs his or her body back for a while!"

As they enter the terminal, Molly asks, "We have no tickets, Moa. How will we get through security to get on the airplane?"

"Watch this." Moa walks up to a security guard and waves her hand across his face.

"Right this way." The male security office opens a special gate and escorts everyone through a metal detector and nods to another as they are allowed to exit.

"That's the fastest I've ever been through a security line." Hillary looks back as the officer returns to his work. "Incredible, Moa. Nicely done. Now where do we go?"

"Over here." Moa leads the group to an empty gate, then she waves her hand over the locked security door to the gangway and it magically opens.

"But, Moa," Molly protests. "There is no plane at this gate."

"That's what you think," Moa says with a twinkle in her eye.

Adem waddles behind everyone and gives a coo of approval.

When they reach the end, they all look out into the tarmac. Molly was correct, it indeed does appear as if there is no plane connected to the gangway.

"Here we are," Moa says proudly. "Get aboard."

"I don't see anything," Molly says.

"Yes," Moa says reassuringly. "But what do you feel?"

"It feels like a plane is here, but clearly, there is no plane." Molly looks frustrated.

"Heidi, do you hear anything?" Moa tenderly asks the girl.

"I...Yes...I hear the low hollowness of enclosed voices. The pilot is talking on his radio." Heidi looks jubilant. "I hear it!"

"Oh, Lord. I see it." Hillary is shocked at her own revelation, "It's a plane alright."

"Who'll be first to embark on our incredible adventure?" Moa asks.

"But there's nothing there," Molly says. "We have these extrasensory gifts, but that doesn't make the airplane real."

"Doesn't it?" Moa asks gently. "By trusting those gifts, you make it real."

Molly anxiously looks out into the tarmac. To the naked eye, there is absolutely no airplane. But, her senses tell her it's there. She can smell the plastic aroma of new airplane fuselage, the stale scent of airplane air, but her eyes show nothing more than a door to the outside with baggage trolleys, workers in orange vests and other planes taxiing down the runway. She inhales slowly and holds her breath, putting one tentative foot forward.

Once again, I am fleeing a situation in which I am fearful of pursuit. The farther I get, the worse I feel about my last conquest. Even though I've only taken and consumed two people's gifts, I am more convinced than ever that I am a victim of circumstances. Surely, I reason, I am not meant for a life of energetic vampirism. In each event, I was forced to act without sufficient preparation. Now, I truly believe, I will use my time and energy more efficiently to find a way to keep myself alive.

The forest is an ideal hiding place and I navigate the stones and twigs more adeptly than my previous trip. As I find a soft cushion of fallen pine branches to lie on, I ponder what will become of poor souls who must live their lives without ever discovering their true gifts? Perhaps, after I am more fully restored to health, I can return to those people and find a way to repay or heal them in some manner.

To assuage my burning guilt, I mentally list the differences between me and a vampire: 1) I am, in no way, changing or transforming my clients into anything other than who they are, 2) my clients are not victims, but are co-conspirators in this exchange (they've agreed to relinquish their gift before I take them), 3) I'm not taking their blood, only their undiscovered gifts. (How can they know what they do not miss?)

I'm beginning to feel better about my actions when a similarity between me and a vampire pops in: I need other people to survive.

Well, in a way, I say to myself, doesn't everyone?

This behavior will change, I tell myself. It has to. I am not a vampire or a cannibal. It is absurd to imagine that I, a kind, loving person, could perform even two such heinous acts, but it stops right here. I will devise a plan to circumvent my current situation and that's that.

Grateful for the newly acquired energy, but still cautious, I resign myself to exploring the forest despite the overwhelming darkness. However, as I do so, I find it increasingly difficult to walk. The feeling is similar to my previous experience in the forest, so I creep closer to the barely lit area just beyond my resting spot. Just as before, my arm is swollen but now, my other arm has joined it in the same state. One of my legs is thick and bloated and my stomach feels like it is being stretched from the inside.

Frightened beyond belief, I now realize that there is a correlation between my gift consuming and my bodily changes.

"You want to know a secret?" A tinny voice rattles my brain.

This is not my own voice, but a strange, metallic version and I stop to make sure I'm not hallucinating. After several seconds of silence, I decide that fear has gotten the best of me and I must need some rest. I settle back down into my soft pine needle nest with my sweltering, swollen, throbbing limbs extended away from my body in hopes of cooling them down..

My forearm skin feels as though it is about to pop and as I touch it, I begin to weep. "This is not me! Not my body!" I cry aloud even though I know no one is there and then I realize it. No one is here. I am completely and utterly isolated. My heart begins to pound and I call out for my father, "Father, please. I need you."

Silence.

Maybe it's best that I die here. Perhaps I was meant to learn that sometimes life involves pain and torture. It is frightening being without the usual voices, the dead ones, my grandmother and my namesake, Yoshimoto. Where are they?

I squeeze my eyes shut and pray for help and my prayer is answered in the form of an insect, perhaps it's a spider, although, in the dark I cannot be completely sure.

For a blessed moment, I am back in my father's embrace. He cradles me after I have fallen from a tree. Drying my tears and holding me close, he tells me a story of a spider.

"We all have incarnations, Minamo." I savor my father's warmth and love as he continues. "You understand that souls choose to come into this world in order to work out the karma, or unfinished business, from other lifetimes."

I press my cheek against his shoulder as he holds me in his arms and rubs my injured knee. Love floods through my being and I pray that I may stay like this with him forever.

He spies a tiny spider crawling and picks it up on his finger. The tiny insect skitters up his index finger toward the cuff of his worn work shirt. "This spider could have been a king, a seamstress or even a farmer like me. Each of us chooses a life, but the man who chooses to come back as the smallest of the small living creatures on Earth has asked for great blessings."

I watch as he moves his sleeve up to a tree limb and lets it climb off to freedom deep within the creases of the bark.

"We all have worldly business to conduct here on Earth, Minamo. Remember that when you find a challenge, look for the gift. That spider will have to face the unknown and perhaps meet many a predator before it finds food and moves forward with its life."

"You mean I chose to be here?" Even though this is a memory, I feel my chest rumble as my voice forms the words.

"Yes. You chose me and Ma. In fact, you chose things that were going to happen to you, chose them in advance while you were in the Great Space." My father places his hand on my heart.

"What Great Space?" I put my hand over his. "Is it in here?"

"The place where all souls go between lives. It is there that you carefully choose your work before you arrive." He smiles. "The Great Space is deep within all of us. Many believe it is heaven and exists in the sky. But, I will share a secret with you. The Great Space is a line, which connects us all as souls. When our souls leave our bodies, we go deeper within our souls where we reconnect with Source."

"If I could do it again, I'd choose an easy life. One with no pain and many riches." I bury my nose in his sleeve and inhale the earthy scent of my father. "That's what I should have done when I chose this lifetime."

"Not me." My father leans his head back against the trunk of the tree and sighs. "I want to progress through my work so that I may become a Celestial Teacher. That is my aim."

My body begins to tremble as it did back then and I snuggle in closer to him. "Please don't leave me. I don't know what I'd do if you went to the Great Place without me."

"Minamo, even if that happens, one day, we will meet again and dance in the light together. Until then, we are here to till the soil of our body, mind and soul."

The memory dissolves in a mist and I am left, lying beneath a blanket of brush and trees, darkness enveloping every particle of my self. A whisper jolts me to attention,

"You want to know a secret?" I shiver as I feel a small insect crawl up my leg. I pray that it's a spider.

CHAPTER XIII
Wandering Attitude

Ritual: Sacred Space
Element: Copper
Planet: Venus

Sacred Space begins with settling the mind. For when your mind is settled it may be deemed sacred.

Find a place to sit quietly where you will be undisturbed for at least twenty minutes. When you are settled, begin with three clearing breaths. Imagine that with each inhale, you bring in light and open energy, and with each exhale you release stale negative energy. After the three breaths, create a clear white space in your mind. Imagine that this space is yours and only yours. No one or nothing may enter unless you wish it so.

Bring your attention to the center of this space and sit there. Allow your imagination to create sights, sounds, scents, feelings and experiences which will enhance your sacred space. Whatever you experience during this ritual is okay. If you see or hear nothing,

that is what your sacred space is to be, for now. You may find that
when you visit another time, your space has changed.
Within the expansion of your unique sacred space, you may be
whoever you wish to be, say whatever you wish to say and you will
experience universal acceptance.

Know that, even when you return to everyday life, your sacred
space is still with you.

Molly takes a deep breath and steps out past the gangway into what she senses is the threshold of the plane. She realizes she must trust herself and what she believes. The minute her foot hits what she senses as the floor, a plane appears! Molly takes another step and is welcomed by a flight attendant dressed in a crisp red uniform.

Meanwhile, in the gangway, Molly has disappeared from view!

"Where'd she go? Mom!" Heidi rushes after her mother and disappears as well.

Hillary takes Adem's thick hand in hers, "Come on Adem. I see it, do you?" Together, they walk through the threshold with Moa close behind and are greeted with a resounding cheer.

"You made it!" Heidi gives her aunt a hug.

"That was incredible." Hillary takes in the beautiful surroundings. They are in a full-sized plane and much to her surprise, they are not alone.

The plane isn't completely filled to capacity, however, many seats have occupants of varying ages, shapes and sizes. At first, Hillary notices a mother and her two children, then she sees a group of teens both male and female listening to music. The more she observes, the more she sees that not everyone is human. There is a man with wings. Is he an angel? Before she can answer her own questions, she sees a woman with blue skin and purple hair. Her eyes are very widely spaced and her nose is incredibly tiny. Then, she notices a filmy green blob with tentacles that are waving gently.

She doesn't feel threatened by these beings. In fact, she almost feels comforted by their presence.

"Welcome to my world!" Moa says proudly. She now appears as her seven year old self.

Hillary is so happy to see Moa's familiar form, she gives her a big hug and is pleased to see she can finally do so! Suddenly she remembers her mother. "What did you do with Mom's body?"

"I gave it back." Moa walks toward the back of the plane to sit with the rest of their group. "She's driving back home. I've implanted the idea that we are safely making our way to our new destination."

Hillary rests her head back on the comfy airplane seat. "Are we off to Japan?"

"Yes." Moa nods.

"Are all of these others going to Japan as well?" Hillary looks out the window as they begin to taxi toward the runway.

"Some are, some aren't," Moa says mysteriously.

"So," Hillary looks around the airplane at the unusual group of passengers. "If we have the power to do this, why are we traveling by plane? Why not just dematerialize as we did in Egypt?"

"Because, your sister, niece and nephew are in temporary physical bodies. They cannot travel that way because they risk separating another body from its original soul as well as their own. This is the ideal transportation for this scenario."

"Oh." Hillary tries to take in the information. "Where are our bodies? Will you help us find them and reintegrate Molly, Heidi and Adem?"

"No." Moa says. "I can only take you to Japan. Your journey must be completed on your own merits and without further help."

"Why?" Hillary asks.

"You are all on a certain path. My intervention has been, thus far, a loophole in the Crone's story. Just as you had to use your gifts to get on this plane, you will be asked to trust forces other than yourselves in order to find Molly's, Heidi's and Adem's bodies and reintegrate their souls. She knows what is happening, but because she made up the rules for her game she must abide by them."

"Moa, you are using the words 'story' and 'game' like they are unreal. But, this situation, it is very real," Hillary says.

"What exactly is real? Your thoughts make whatever you perceive to be real. Beyond that, what exists?" Moa says.

"But you said that Molly, Heidi and Adem are in danger. What else am I to think? Isn't the danger real?" Hillary asks.

"Yes. Because you all have agreed that it is. You have all traveled down a path which has created this situation, just as the Crone has, and you must now watch it play out. Hillary, evil is as you perceive it to be. Remember that as you try to find and retrieve that which you deserve. Be careful of your thoughts, Hillary. It is with our thoughts that we manifest reality. For now, you should rest. You have a long trip ahead and you might not have time to sleep once we land." Moa puts a hand on Hillary's shoulder, and she instantly falls into a deep, restful sleep.

Just before Hillary falls asleep, she wonders what would cause the Crone to desire to harm her, her sister, niece and nephew. Then, slipping into a languid sleep, she dreams that the thought gives her ability to fly and observe herself at the same time. She watches her body pull away from herself in the airplane seat and soar through the misty clouds. Swooping lower, she remembers the Crone's words to her before Hillary appeared on the plane to Los Tardos, "You have bigger fish to fry."

What did the Crone mean by that? Why would Hillary help someone who desires to harm her and her family? Hillary finds a pocket of air and is instantly sucked through a dark portal and lands with a plop in a dark, heavy-feeling place. Where is she? Her limbs feel leaden, her body aches and she feels such sadness. Opening her eyes, she is shocked to find herself back in the examination room in which she had her first "in body" experience. She glances down at her bitten nails, her tiny hands and her tattoo. Why is she here again? The hopelessness is overwhelming and she tries to cry out, but cannot. Tears begin to stream down her cheeks as she attempts, in vain, to pull her wrists through the thick leather restraints. If there was a version of hell on earth, she thinks, this is it. Imagine being trapped in this body for eternity. Imagine trying to escape, cry out, seek help and never, ever finding resolution. Suddenly, she wants to leave. She wills herself to get out of the body, but she cannot. She is stuck here. Stuck in this horrible situation and it isn't even hers!

Panic sets in and she thrashes her worn body, trying to escape. The thoughts! She was thinking about the Crone and her evil nature, and those thoughts brought her back here. But why?

In the blackness of my new home, I try to discern whether the voice is inside my head or coming from somewhere else. Either way, I decide that my best option is to answer the barely audible voice that I am hoping is a spider.

"Uh, yes. I do wish to know a secret." Anything is better than being alone, I say to myself.

"Very well." It is a small voice. Quiet and reed thin with a tinny timbre at the end.

Suddenly, the tree on which my head is resting cracks open and sucks my entire body into its hollow. I tumble backwards, head over heels and summersault, landing with a plunk right at the feet of a tiny, hooded druid.

"You thought you were alone deep in the forest. Didn't you?" She giggles a sweet titter.

Before I can answer, this wee druid—no bigger than a baby rabbit—clatters in and sits down on a tiny moss bench with a harrumph.

Two more robed druids with hoods pulled up to cover their tiny faces, come into the small sparsely decorated room and barely acknowledge any of us as they speak animatedly about a recent occurrence. It is obviously important to them, although it is still not evident why the issue is so important.

The largest druid pulls out a small copper wand and points it at a large clock behind her, which instantly lets out an incredibly loud BONG.

All in attendance are quiet and the main druid begins to intone:

"We call in the Great Witch to invoke the Seven Noble Metals of the Ancients." She points the wand down at the earth and turns in a circle while saying, "Copper, Gold, Iron, Lead, Silver, Tin and Electrum."

A green light engulfs the main druid, her tiny feet dig into the earth and she begins to vibrate. Through her, an odd, low voice rumbles, "Our lesson is on manifesting alternative reality through sacred ritual."

The others look on as the odd scene plays out. I cannot understand what is happening and I gape at our tiny druid teacher vibrating and emitting a green light. One of the students notices my confused look and scoots closer to me. "She is channeling. That is when we call in the forces of The Great Witch and she speaks through us."

"Can all of you do that?" It is hard to imagine having someone else speak through me.

"No. Not all of us. We have to be activated."

"How does that happen?" Despite my worry, I am curious.

"When this lesson is over, you can ask the teacher if you are worthy of being activated."

"Worthy?"

"Only some people get to be channelers. Only some possess the correct balance of skills and humility."

An unknown force begins to tickle the top of my head. It is annoying and I try to bat it away. Then I notice something strange about my classmates. Each one seems to be suffering in some way. The two druids who came in together both have red pustules which seem to get bigger and bigger as the teacher speaks. The other druid looks like he is in severe pain. I observe my own distended abdomen that matches my right leg and arm, which are red and puffy, the skin tight and uncomfortably warm.

The teacher continues in her low rumbling tone, "When creating a ritual, you must remember three things: Structure, Setup and Safety. Every ritual has a structure and although you are free to make that structure work any way you desire, it is essential that you remain consistent with your structure. Before you perform your ritual, you must set an intention to do no harm. If you begin with your thoughts toward a positive outcome, you will create a powerful ritual. Lastly, since we are all extremely powerful, we must take great care in protecting ourselves and those around us from harm during these rituals."

"If you leave even one of these items out, you risk not only directing the power in an undesirable way toward yourself but toward others, too, and that will defeat the purpose of doing a ritual. The key to a powerful ritual is clear sight, not just with the eyes, but more importantly, with your intuition. You must have crystal clear intuitive sight in order to focus your ritual's intent. We will now learn by doing. Specifically, with a core learning ritual, called 'Relax the Third Eye.'"

"Bring your attention to the center of your skull," the teacher whispers. "You're about to go on a magnificent journey within yourself."

CHAPTER XIV

Unused Gifts

Ritual: Relax the Third Eye
Element: Tin
Planet: Jupiter

The purpose of this ritual is simple. Clear your intuitive sight center which is located between the brows, deep within your head. This is the place where you sense the unexplainable, gather ideas from the ether and receive messages without the aid of sight, sound or touch. The most important thing to remember while performing this ritual is to clear your mind of any negative thoughts which can derail even the most honored ritual.

Find a place where you will be undisturbed and sit in silence, with eyes closed, for six breaths. As you inhale and exhale, remember that you are not only a body, but you are also a soul. After the sixth breath, imagine that a column of light extends from the heavens, through the top of your head and out into the ground below you which connects to the center of the earth.

Now, imagine a gold halo encircles the area just above the top of your head. This gold halo has the power to increase your inner strength and intuitive power.

Say the following as you visualize the halo sending healing relaxing energy into your third eye, the center of your head. Breathe in the centering, calming energy and sit within the comforting energy for as long as you wish.

When you feel completely full, thank yourself for your efforts and open your eyes.

You will know all the sacred information as you need to, you will understand all there is to life when you are ready, you will experience the desires you wish when it is time.

Blessed Be.

The plane has begun its descent into Tokyo and all passengers ready themselves for arrival. Arms stretch, tentacles wave and Moa smiles at Hillary's peacefully sleeping countenance. It almost seems a shame to wake her after such a nice nap.

"Wake up, Hillary." Moa gently jostles her shoulder. But Hillary does not respond and Moa instantly understands.

"Molly." Moa calls her over and says, "We have a slight change of plans. You are now looking for three bodies and one soul."

"What?" Molly looks at Hillary and back at Moa, "Hillary, wake up!" She shakes her sister's shoulder but gets no response.

"What happened?" Molly says. "Is she ill? Has she been drugged?"

"No." Moa says. "It's complicated but suffice it to say, her Ka went traveling again and we need to locate it as well. For the meantime, I'll keep her body safe here while you all search for your own physical bodies and Hillary's energetic body."

"How on earth do I find that?" Molly asks anxiously. "Do you have any idea where she is?"

"I have an idea of who she is…" Moa says, "but not where."

"Who she is? What does that mean?" Molly's voice is getting an edge to it. "You mean she's in another person's body?"

"Yes," Moa says solemnly. "I believe she is inside the Crone's body."

"B…but, isn't the Crone dead. Didn't she die hundreds of years ago?" Molly sits down.

"Time is relative. Just because you're looking for someone doesn't mean you need to limit yourself to time."

"Do you have a time capsule or something?" Molly asks hopefully.

"No. But you do," Moa says.

"I don't follow," Molly says.

"Let's get off the plane and I'll do my best to find another loophole."

"A what?" Molly asks.

"Never mind," Moa says as the plane's wheels touch the tarmac and the aircraft comes to a smooth stop. As the plane taxis into the gate, Moa adds, "I may not be able to help you find Hillary or your bodies, but I can educate you on the rules of the game."

Moa calls the group to the back of the plane and explains, "I will not leave this plane because it is imperative to stay with Hillary's body. However, here is what you need to do to find your own bodies and Hillary's ka. Think of your journey as a game and remember every game has rules.

"There are only three rules for your body/ka finding game. First, you must stay on track. Keep your goal of finding your bodies and Hillary's Ka as a singular goal. The Crone may try to throw you off your game by distracting you from your desired result. Don't let her do it!

"Second, do not agree to anything you don't wish to manifest. The Crone is a master at manipulation. As you recall, she got Ku to agree to let her steal his cherished healing gifts.

"Third, and this is the most important rule of all, under no circumstances, should you allow the Crone to derail your thoughts. Thoughts create a portal through which you may travel to the light or dark. Keep your thoughts positive and hopeful and you'll stay in the light. If you find yourself thinking negative or destructive thoughts, that is most likely the Crone intervening in your mission. I will be waiting here, and when you are finished, return here and we will celebrate your victory!"

"Molly," Moa says, looking carefully at her, "What do you sense about the location of your body? And what about Heidi's and Adem's body and Hillary's ka?"

"Our bodies are most likely located at the Chansyn-burabura Corporation in Kamakura, Japan. Hillary feels like she is being held captive in an office as well, but not at the corporation. More like a medical building. But how can that be? The Crone's body is long dead which means it no longer exists."

"Remember to keep your thoughts positive," Moa reminds kindly.

"I hear the sound of traffic and a faint noise of trash trucks. Also, water is dripping like rain," Heidi says.

"So it's raining," Molly interjects.

"Not necessarily. Broaden your scope of thinking." Moa pauses, then says, "Okay. You have enough information to begin. Your transportation is outside of baggage claim. A man named Toshi will escort you to your desired location. Now go! There is no time to waste!"

Molly takes Heidi's and Adem's hands and steps off of the plane into the gangway. "Let's find Toshi."

The group exits the terminal at baggage claim and Heidi spies a slim man with dark hair who is holding a sign with "Ka Rescue Team" on it.

"At least Moa is able to keep her sense of humor," Molly says wryly as they all pile into the silver sedan.

The car pulls out of the airport and heads onto an access road which leads around the neon lights and tall buildings of Tokyo.

"How far away is Kamakura?" Heidi asks.

Toshi looks into the rear view mirror at Heidi. "It's about an hour south of here. Sit back and relax, Heidi. We'll be there in no time. Before you know it, we'll be in Kamakura."

Molly chuckles to herself.

"What is it, Mom?" Heidi asks.

"I was just trying to picture what my body is doing without 'me' inside." Molly pauses then adds, "I can only imagine."

"I don't know anything about Kamakura," Heidi sighs. "Can you fill me in on the particulars, Toshi?"

"Sure. In 1158 Minamoto Yoritomo became the first shogunate of Japan. Within a year, however, the Minamoto clan lost the Hogen War and Yoritomo was put in exile for twenty years. Upon his return to Kamakura, he attempted to reestablish a military government and succeeded. Yoritomo became gravely ill and died in 1199. The Morimoto clan was beset with tragedy after tragedy following Yorimoto's untimely death and his eldest son was assassinated, then his second son was put to death after murdering his uncle. It is said that the Morimoto lineage was ended after the second son's death. But, legend has it that one girl survived (because women were not counted in genealogy back then) and Morimoto's vow to right the wrongs committed by his children continues to this very day as his soul is reincarnated time and time again."

"The poor Minamoto clan," Heidi says. "Does anyone know who his current reincarnation is?"

"There is a story about that as well," Toshi says in a mysterious tone. "I've heard that the last surviving Minamoto soul got stuck when she was a little girl. The story goes that she went to Minamoto Yoritomo's shrine in an attempt to pay homage, but instead was cursed for past life wrongs. She never had a chance, poor dear."

"What was her name?" Molly asks.

"Minamoto," Toshi replies. "There are no records of her existence after the age of ten. Many people believe the lineage should die as it was doomed to tragedy and strife, but I think there is still hope for them."

The sedan pulls up in front of a brand new office building in the midst of an enormous office park. The group gets out and takes in the twelve-story high structure adorned with glass and steel.

"Looks pretty swanky," Heidi says.

"Gambagoo!" Adem replies.

"Thanks, Toshi." Molly turns back to the car, but it is nowhere in sight. "Well, it looks like we'll have to figure out our return trip after we find ourselves, so to speak."

Heidi leads the way and the group enters a glass door leading to a beautifully decorated lobby with granite floors and security desks as well as two extra long overstuffed leather couches.

"Hi." A young woman behind the desk is dressed in a security guard uniform. She nods to the group.

"Hi. We're here to see…" Molly searches for a name and blurts out, "Minamoto."

The guard looks blankly at Molly and shakes her head.

"Oh, she doesn't speak English," Molly says.

Suddenly, Adem steps forward and in perfect Japanese, asks for Minamoto!

I t is inside this tree that I learn all there is to know about creating magic, manifesting my desires and clearing myself of my own rotten-to-the-core appetites.

I find pride in my actions, for I never harm any of my classmates, nor my teacher. Instead, I am able to sustain my existence by creating rituals. I create rituals for protection, for invoking inner wisdom and slowly begin to heal myself.

This tree becomes my safe place and I flourish with the aid of my teacher and classmates. We work endlessly, tirelessly, perfecting our craft to ensure that our manifestations of reality are clear and flawless. Time ceases to exist during our work and I gratefully watch as my arm and leg return to their normal state.

Once each of us has completed our first full ritual, the druid teacher calls us together.

"It is time for you all to take the sacred vow of the Great Witch. Please come forward one at a time, to receive your strands of Moldavite." She holds up a beautiful glimmering necklace made of bright green glowing jewels.

"Mina," she calls, and I step forward and bow as she speaks. "This necklace holds with it a powerful connection to the Universe. You have cleared your consciousness of clutter by purifying it with celestial fire. You have washed your ego with the salt show ceremony. Now, with the completion of your first ritual, "Relaxing the Third Eye," the Great Witch has asked that you receive this necklace which will shatter your current reality and allow you to access higher dimensional celestial frequencies. These stones were created when a meteor hit the Earth fifteen million years ago and will aid in your spiritual evolution."

As she places the necklace, I feel a rush of heat flow outward from my head to my feet and my heart pounds as if I've been running. I catch my breath and she continues. "Mina, do you vow to keep sacred those lessons you have learned during your time with the group, to bring forth your healing without harming another?"

Suddenly, the heat forms a cord around my throat and I feel suffocated. I cannot speak, but images of those people whose gifts I stole and consumed begin to flash rapid-fire in my mind. In my mind's eye, I see them slumbering peacefully, then their quiet murmurs of agreement and eventually, my self-satisfied grin.

I lower my head, careful to hide my eyes from her steady gaze, her judgmental stare presses on my vocal cords as I attempt, in vain, to breathe deeply. Then looking up, daring her to deny my birthright, my healing, my own power, I whisper, "Yes."

Then the real hell begins.

What I don't realize is that a vow such as the one I've just taken is not done lightly. In fact, immediately upon my agreement, a funny thing happens. A deep, burning hunger ignites in my belly, the likes of which I have never experienced in this life or in any other, and I regret my agreement the second it exits my lips.

The floor doesn't open up and blood doesn't seep down the walls. No, this is a private hell. One can only experience a hell like this when one has taken a wrong turn, made a cosmic misstep and embarked on an irrevocable, one-way journey to a new and unanticipated, uncharted destination.

As I watch my classmates receive their necklaces and affirm their vows, my gnawing hunger pulls at my insides and I wonder if anyone has noticed my reaction to this initiation. When the final vow is taken, the druid teacher reveals a gleaming crystal ball nestled in a bed of moss. With thoughts as our guide, we are told to look into the crystal ball to divine our next journey—where we are most needed. As I gaze into the shimmering ball, a picture begins to emerge of a young boy with tremendous gifts who sits alone on a rock in Egypt. My intuition tells me he will soon be killed if I do not intervene.

Then the druid teacher says, "Wherever you are called is your destiny. Your vow to the Great Witch binds you to this calling and your task at hand. If you do not complete your task, not only will you die, but those who you have sought to help will also perish."

For a moment, I worry that I will not be up to the task of helping this boy. My fears are put to rest when I realize that this is finally a perfect opportunity to do good for once! I vow to move heaven and earth to save this boy's life.

As my teacher suggests, I ask the Great Witch to facilitate my trip and I suddenly feel the dirt floor opening up beneath my feet. It feels like quicksand and instantly I am enveloped in darkness. The blackness feels liquid and thick as if I'm flowing within a river of mud and then I emerge in a desert next to a large stone temple.

This is not the location I saw in my vision. In my mind's eye, I have seen the boy sitting on a rock meditating, but I decide that I can do my work from here. I will try to save the boy from harm despite the gnawing hunger that is within my body. The hunger becomes like a voice inside, and it screams at me to take his gift, but I know otherwise. I do a ritual in which I relax my mind's eye and clear the hunger feelings, then I focus on finding a way to save this little boy's life. In my initiation, I vowed to help this boy and I will not stop until I finish my task. Failure, my druid teacher promised, will include death to me as well as to the boy, so I must not fail.

Just as I settle in, the ground begins to shake and a large cloud appears, out of which emerges a muscular man. "You are the stealer of gifts! I cannot allow you to do more harm."

Surprised that he knows me I ask, "Who are you?"

"I am the King of Jupiter. You have been given many lifetimes of chances to conquer your fears and yet you have continually chosen the low road. The lower vibrational emotions have molded you into a person who is driven by her desires and not by a desire to help mankind."

"But I have learned to love and do good, why don't you see that? The Great Witch says..."

"The Great Witch made a pact to collect all initiates' unused gifts, Mina. White Witches were as misguided as you were. When you signed on with them, they did as you had done and relieved your being of every last gift you had." He interrupts, "Since you are unable to cease your endless cycle of horror, I shall do so for you."

"I have been wronged! Everywhere I go, people are afraid of me, they misunderstand my actions. I am a good person. Why do people not see this?" My anger creates a roiling cloud around my head and body. "Even a stranger comes to me as if I am a danger to others. It was me who was wronged. Me! If I was put on this earth to do good, I certainly wasn't given the chance. Instead, I was forced to survive, left to rot in a room barely escaping death."

"I have news for you, Mina. You are already dead," the King says sadly.

"No. I visited the knitting woman, the girls who taunted me. They were real," I scream at him. Then I look down at my arms and legs. They are withered and old. My hair hangs in strings of silver and black and extends almost to my waist.

"Your body is still in the acupuncturists office. He and his staff fled the office and locked you in and never returned. Your body is there, withering away, Your soul has taken flight and you, Mina, you couldn't access your body even if you tried. You are stuck between the worlds. I am here to ensure that you do harm to no one else. You will agree to come with me to Jupiter."

Rage fills my being and I scream, "No! How can I be dead! After all my hard work? My trials, I am stuck here?" Then I let out a howl and summon my last reserve of energy, willing it to transport me back to my young self so I may warn her of what might become of her if she does not change her path. I call in the Great Witch to send for time and space travel so I may return to Japan and stop myself from agreeing to the heinous King's wishes. I am granted the ability to travel back in time, circling through my life until I stand beside myself as a young girl. Seeing this scene from long ago at the Minamoto Shrine in Japan unfold is enough to push my fury to peak force. I will not allow her to listen to this tyrant King. In desperation, I show her the withered old crone she may become, I desperately warn her of the impending doom which may befall her if she follows the King to Jupiter.

My young self looks on in terror and recoils from my efforts to convert her to my side, so I battle the King alone, with every bit of strength I have left.

But, he is stronger, he shrinks the Iron Shinto, envelopes me in his portal and sends me back to Egypt, next to the temple. I have been drained of all power and begin to howl at the sky, "Why did this happen to me? Why me?"

The temple begins to shake and its foundation begins to crumble and the King silences me with a wave of his strong hand. "You have no idea of your power, Mina, and that is what makes you so dangerous. It is the manner in which you use it that drains you so. I have brought the Iron Shinto here and will place you within it so you may contemplate your place in life, your location, as it were. Perhaps you will not harm others if you have time to think about the consequences caused by stealing others' gifts."

"But the boy…" I can only manage a mumble because the King's silencing power has taken most of my voice away. "He was here…"

"A mirage. He will be here in a thousand or so years. For now, rest, dear Mina. You have much to think about."

The King calls forth an energy block which encases my physical and energetic body and renders me powerless and then transports me into the basement of the temple. The King has placed the Iron Shinto within this temple and created a room, which will be my prison. He places chains on my wrists and ankles with heavy electromagnetic cuffs, from which I cannot move. "But," I can only manage a whisper, "I was trying to survive. I didn't want to hurt those people."

The gnawing hunger becomes a desperate yawning hole and I pray over and over for it to be filled. Failure at not completing my mission to find and secure Minamoto's inner voice claws at my throat. I cannot fail at my vow to ensure the boy's safety.

Years upon years, I pray for help, but none comes. Occasionally, I try to escape, but the cuffs are so heavy, I end up being bruised and battered. Hundreds of years go by, I am ravenous, but I wither and remain in my undead state. As the hunger eats away at me, my unending rage blossoms into a fury. Revenge is all I can think about as I plot my escape. Surely there is a way to find the boy and lure him to me. That, I realize is my only way of escape.

CHAPTER XV

Thought Wrangler

Ritual: Thought Wrangler
Element: Copper
Planet: Venus

Sit in a comfortable position and relax with three breaths. Begin to see your thoughts as individual bubbles in a never-ending stream. This stream flows by you and contains all the thoughts in the universe. Imagine that it is your job to pick your own thoughts out of this universal stream. As thoughts appear in your head ask yourself if each thought is worthy of existing within your mind. You determine the worth and value of each thought by knowing that thoughts create your reality.

Bring your awareness to this stream and say:
Blessed are the thoughts which flow into my mind and blessed are the thoughts which flow away from my mind. I am not my thoughts, I can choose to connect with or release any thoughts which flow by and I know that the thoughts I choose create my reality.

Shocked that Adem suddenly spouts out Japanese to the security guard, Molly and Heidi gape at him. Meanwhile, the guard has pushed a button to allow the group to access the elevator.

Adem waddles over and hits the up arrow with his palm. Then as they enter the elevator, he presses all the buttons!

"We don't have time for this!" Molly is annoyed. "Adem. We are not on all of these floors."

"Wait!" Heidi says quietly. "Maybe we are."

Heidi scans the lit buttons then says to Molly, "Okay, I'll hold the door open and you search each floor. That way we will maximize our time."

The elevator reaches the first floor and Molly exits, quickly searching through a large mezzanine with a coffee shop and restaurant setup. She soon returns. "This isn't it."

The second through tenth floors are offices and corridors. However, the eleventh floor is filled with cubicles covered in blue fabric.

"I have a good feeling about this...," Hillary says as she dashes out of the elevator to explore.

As she walks down each aisle, Molly looks over walls, through openings for her body. No one notices as she walks stealthily through the aisles perusing the people at work. She returns to the elevator and they rise to the final floor.

This floor has cubicles as well, but all are lined with green fabric.

"Someone could have been away from her desk, I suppose," Molly says as she returns from a quick perusal. "Let's go back to the eleventh floor and I'll do another round."

They do so, but Molly scours the eleventh floor, looking in and around each blue fabric cubicle to no avail.

Finally, she returns and says to Heidi and Adem, "You know Moa said something about the Crone trying to deceive us by messing with our thoughts. Do you think she could have…" Molly gets in the elevator and pushes twelve. Upon exiting, the fabric on the twelve floor cubicles has now changed to yellow. "Why that…" Molly presses the elevator close button and then immediately opens the doors with the button. The cubicle fabric on the twelfth floor is now blue. Molly dashes into the sea of cubicles, determined to find her body.

As she walks through the aisle once more and this time, concentrates on what she remembers about her location. When she sat in the plane and came up with a visual of what her body saw in front of herself, it was as follows: male with dark curly hair, blue fabric, can only see the back of people's heads…

A single desk, something she'd missed on her first go around on this floor, sits in an offset cubicle. It has a low wall in front, but on both sides are two high walls. That explains why, when they were divining information, Hillary was only able to see the back of people's heads.

There, with a blank expression, is Molly's body. Her face is pale and her eyes are bloodshot and she sits in front of a computer monitor. As Molly approaches her body, she senses a tremendous amount of weariness and fear—in fact, a field of fear surrounding the entire cubicle. Molly's body has been held captive by this "fear field."

Examining the fear field, Molly notices a pattern. Since Molly's body has an emotional memory, the field attaches to past negative experiences and brings them to the present. Molly can sense that upon her approach, her body remembers a time when, at a past job, a female co-worker tried to get her fired. The co-worker did her best to talk behind Molly's back, derail her projects and undermine her authority. The memory is so strong, that it became a part of Molly's body and was housed at the base of her skull. Molly can feel the base of her skull pulsing with anxiety as it feeds a cord which connects to the fear field.

Molly senses that her even though she's been placed here temporarily, her body has taken on the fears of a new female co-worker who is somewhere in the sea of cubicles. Closing her eyes, she can feel the present-day work situation and the female co-worker's anger and fear flooding Molly's fear field every few minutes with pounding negative thoughts.

Oddly, Molly's body found this job because it thought the situation offered safety and security until her Ka could be returned. However, her co-worker has tapped into Molly's body's past fears and Molly has now mistaken this woman's fear for her own. The reality, as Molly further examines the field, is that the co-worker is merely being herself—thinking negative thoughts, spreading gossip and hatred is just who she is and what she does. Molly's body is mistaking the woman's negativity for her own and has been trying to work the fear out to no avail.

Molly whispers to her body, "I know how to get you out of here. But, you have to trust me and keep your thoughts positive."

Her body gives a tired nod and continues to look at the monitor as she says, "I'll never get out of here."

"First, you must believe you are safe. It may be hard to believe given the circumstances, but you can..." Molly realizes she will never get her body out of this cubicle unless she cuts off the external negativity first.

So, she wanders through the sea of cubicles, feeling the pulse at the back of her skull increase then slightly decrease. As her guide, she uses the pulsing pain to lead her to the woman. And she finds herself directly in front of a moon-faced gnome of a woman. The woman is seated about three rows up and four rows away from Molly's body's desk.

The woman doesn't look up as Molly sits at the chair directly in front of the woman. "You have a choice," Molly says evenly. "You can either stop sending hatred to Molly or you can relinquish your Feeling Projection Power which will keep you from sending negativity to any other human being again. I'll give you three seconds to decide."

"I'm just doing my job." The woman gives Molly a haughty look.

"Maybe so," Molly says. "And now your job, as you know it, stops. You will no longer gossip, defame, derail or mess with Molly."

The squat woman rises from her chair. "Who are you?"

"I'm an advocate for those who have been harmed by you." Molly continues to keep her voice calm. "You're done spreading hatred and negativity. Will you stop? Yes or no."

"No." The woman stands defiantly at her desk.

"Oh, look. Molly looks at the clock on her desk." Molly says. "Your time is up. From now on, everyone will know your true intentions."

Molly rises and smiles. "Have a nice day."

As she returns to her body's cubicle, she hears the computers on the desks indicating receipt of a new email from the mean woman. They've all received a nasty, gossip-filled email meant for one co-worker. In it, the woman implicates herself in quite a few rumors.

Her body's eyes widen with recognition and Molly smiles, "You're free. Let's go."

With her right hand, Molly reaches into the waning fear field and slices the cord at the base of her body's skull. Then, she ties off the end closest to her head and seals it off with protective light. Molly escorts her body back to the elevator bank where Heidi and Adem are waiting.

Heidi is holding the door open and gasps when she sees her mother's body! "Mom!"

"Well, not yet." Molly says, We're not quite integrated." Then Molly turns to her body, "Where are Heidi and Adem's bodies?"

Still afraid, Molly's body speaks in a whisper, "They're in the daycare."

"I don't need a daycare!" Heidi proclaims.

"Okay, let's go. And don't worry, you're safe. We've got security with us." Molly gives Adem and Heidi a wry smile.

The group heads down the elevator and out the lobby and main entrance to another small building.

As they walk, Molly, still in Krystal's body says, "We're going to need Moa's help with our reintegration."

Finally, my day comes. I hear the stir of the sand above my head. I relish the feeling of knowing that the boy, Ku, I hear he is called, is near. I will soon be fed.

The prophecy has come true. I'm a crone. My soul has drawn up into itself and has become charged with anger. Long forgotten are the healing rituals and positive energy. Instead I wallow in my mistakes, misfortune and bad luck. For these thousand years of imprisonment, I've wallowed in my own desperation to escape from this dank hole. Now, I lie in wait. A roiling, festering mass of pustules and appendages is what I've become. Ku, I've decided, will feed me with his gifts and if we die, we die together. This is my "self."

It is that self which takes over and listens as Ku, walks to his special perch atop a rock and meditates. He is small, but, I can smell his gifts almost taste them. I've craved them now for a thousand years.

I am sure he will come when I call. He is proud and longs to use his healing gifts. His meditation starts and I feel him access my realm. My dimension is within the physical world and the conscious realm. When I feel he can hear me, I begin to call, "Help me! Please! Somebody help!"

Within moments he is at my side and speaking to me with a soothing voice. His agreement to help me is all I need to free me from the chains, which have bound me for eons. His youthful light sickens me and his resilient loving heart feeds my burgeoning jealousy. Who is he to live in the Light when I have had so much darkness?

Without a trace of regret, I plunge my bony arm into his chest and retrieve my bounty. Gobbling his luscious gift gives me more pleasure than I have ever known and I savor its delicious, youthful vivacity. As has happened in the past, my body changes. However, I have never experienced anything like this transformation. So glad to be free am I that I scarcely notice the bulbous pus filled boils, which sprout from my torso or the oozing gunk—evidence of the thousands of years of self-hatred and pity which have overtaken my being—pouring from what once were my eyes, nose and mouth.

I revel in the freedom and send my power in the form of fury out into every person who harmed me. Traveling to the Great Witch who stole my unused gifts I blow a gale so strong through her branches that it unearths the roots and topples the trees. Then on to the Unibrow and the knitting woman who tortured me and taunted me, I flood their minds with a cacophony of emotions and thoughts, short-circuiting their brains. Next, I go back in time and send my rage coursing through the acupuncturist. Then on to the mean boy from my hometown, I send my anger in the form of whispers all around him, taunting him with uncertainty.

Finally, I release a slow burn of ire into my mother as she stands with her fists clenched on our front stoop.

It is then that I turn from her and look at myself walking up the path, the kind police office at my back escorting me home from my adventure at the Temple of Hachiman and the Iron Shinto.

I sense the grief, hurt, anger and even rage I had as a young girl, returning home to a mother who seethed with her own rage.

It was me who created and perpetuated this cycle of anger and continued to feed it with my own downward spiral of negativity. Every choice I made led me to this place and I am forever doomed to repeat this cycle unless I take action to stop myself.

CHAPTER XVI

Interdimensional Travel

Ritual: Relativity Scan
Element: Gold
Planet: Saturn

*Find a stone that will fit in the palm of your hand. Stand, arm
extended and parallel to the ground, with the rock in hand and say:
My reality is mine. I choose to know it and embrace my world and
its reality as a positive, honest, truth giving and receiving realm.
There are certain truths to which I am committed and trust that
I am safe. As this rock falls, I scan my body, mind and spirit for
that which falls outside of my reality.*

*Drop the stone onto the ground and say:
I release that which is not mine back to Source. I am complete.*

The entrance to the daycare is locked and Molly waves to the woman to let her inside. When they all enter, they see Heidi's body lying on a pink bean-bag and Adem snuggled softly in a corner crib.

Molly, still in Krystal's body, attempts to rush to her children's side, but is stopped by a stern-looking woman holding a clipboard. Only Molly's body holds the company identification card, which will allow her children to be retrieved. Molly's body shows the ID, signs the exit form for Adem and Heidi on the clipboard and they all leave the daycare center..

The first person they see upon exiting the building is Toshi who is standing in front of his sedan smiling. "Ready to go?"

"We've got to find Hillary," Molly responds to Toshi as she ushers everyone into the car.

As soon as Toshi pulls out of the parking lot Molly senses that something is wrong. "Toshi. Is there a location in Kamakura where it rains more than normal?"

The driver does not speak, but smiles at her in the rear-view mirror.

"Toshi, we'd like to get out," Molly says sternly. "Please stop."

"But mom," Heidi says. "We need to find Aunt Hillary."

Molly has a sinking feeling that Moa's warning about the Crone taking on other forms has come true.

"Okay," Molly says. "What do you want with us?"

Toshi scowls and an unearthly voice emerges from his unmoving mouth. "It's never wise to question a leader."

"Who says you're a leader?" Molly says.

"I've got the wheel." The driver turns onto a ramp and rolls through a forest and onto a one-lane road.

Signs mark the road in Japanese. However, Heidi whispers to her mother, "We're at Minamoto Yoritomo's shrine."

"That's right, dear Heidi." Again, the voice emanates from somewhere in the driver's chest. "You are being escorted back to the Iron Shinto, the portal to nowhere."

"What?" Molly is incredulous, "That's ridiculous. The Ancient book we retrieved from the King and Queen of Jupiter's home said that the Iron Shinto is a Pyramid Conveyance Structure, which allows interdimensional travel."

"You don't think I would spend thousands of years in that thing without altering it for my own benefit, do you?" A horrid cackle emanates from Toshi's chest.

"But why would you care about us?" Heidi asks.

The driver stops in front of a long stretch of stairs and Heidi gasps, "I see tall guardians! They're all dressed up. Incredible."

The group is escorted out of the car and behind the steps through the door of the now life-sized Iron Shinto.

When they've all entered into the Iron Shinto, the Crone relinquishes Toshi's body and, in a daze, he walks back to his car and departs, unaware that his passengers are now trapped.

The Crone steps through the wall as if it was not there! She immediately zaps Molly, Adem and Heidi's bodies and they fall to the floor in a deep sleep. "Here is what you will do. You will agree to give me your gifts, your clairsenscience and your clairaudience in exchange for Hillary being returned safely to you. I've just put your bodies to sleep, but I will kill them if you do not agree." The Crone's form flickers and fades, then completely disappears.

"She needs us," Molly, in Krystal's body, says. "There's got to be some way to bargain with her."

"I'm scared, Mommy." Heidi, still in the form of the pink-haired teen, runs to and embraces Molly.

"We have to stay positive," Molly says. "I think she needs us and her energy is waning. Didn't you see her image flickering? Remember Moa said stay positive. If we fall into fear, we risk missing an important clue to a solution."

"Moa did say that this is just a game." Heidi brightens. "What if we treated this like a game? The three rules were: Stay on track with our goal. Don't agree to anything she asks. Keep thoughts positive."

"The one thing we know is that she needs us, so she will not harm us until we find our bodies." Molly says. "I just wish we had some outside help. Heidi, how did you know that there were guardians on the steps to Minamoto's Shrine?"

"I heard them talking. They said 'We are the Guardians.' " Heidi says this in a matter-of-fact tone.

"It can't hurt to try and find them." Molly is thinking aloud. "Okay, Heidi. Let's work together. I sense that these Guardians can help us if we ask. But we need to use the right words, almost like a password."

Just then, a strong wind blows through the bars of the Shinto and Heidi gives a shiver. "Oh, I hope it doesn't rain." She says looking at some dark clouds moving toward the park.

"What did Moa say about rain?" Molly asks. "Broaden your scope of thinking. Okay, I think I've got it. Heidi I'm going to address the Guardians. Will you tell me their response?"

"Sure," Heidi says.

"Great Guardians who stand on the steps of Minamoto Yoritomo's Shrine. Please help us to broaden the scope of our thinking so we may reach a positive outcome with the Crone." Molly's voice trails off into the air. Then she waits.

After a moment, Heidi reports, "One is saying he can help, but we must first let go of false beliefs."

"False beliefs…what could that be…" Molly thinks, then says, "Tell him we relinquish our belief that the Crone is more powerful than we because she is not human."

Heidi laughs. "The Guardian says you are very clever. Now the female Guardian asks you for a sacrifice."

"I place my ego on the shrine, for it does me no further good."

"The female Guardian agrees," Heidi says. "The final Guardian would like Adem."

"What?" Molly is horrified. "No. I'll give of myself, but I will not sacrifice another. Especially a child. Absolutely not."

Heidi looks pensive then says, "She says you are not the child's mother, so why do you care what happens to him."

"Because love isn't something I create, it is something given to me. Love is a precious gift and I have nothing to do with its origin, but I have everything to do with its continuation."

Suddenly, the Iron Shinto begins to shake and the door opens to reveal a long tiled hallway with many doors. Molly peers out through the door looking both ways before returning to the group. "It doesn't look like the building we were in."

"Creepy." Heidi shudders. "I hear water dripping. Hey, water dripping! That's what I heard when I thought of Aunt Hillary! Let's go." Thinking nothing of her own safety, Heidi steps out of the Iron Shinto and makes a left, trying every door. Several are empty treatment rooms.

"This must be a medical facility. Why would Hillary be here?" Molly says looking into an empty office directly in front of them..

Heidi tries the last door in the hall next to a window with rusting iron bars.

Molly wiggles the doorknob. "It's deadbolted with a key. I'm sure there is a set of keys somewhere. Maybe we could check this empty office."

As they return to the office, Heidi says, "It is strange that the building is empty."

"It's midnight," Molly says looking at a wall clock on the desk. "I'm sure everyone is gone."

"Why would Hillary still be here if everyone is gone?"

"Is this what I think it is?" Molly looks into the top drawer of the worn dresser and picks up a keychain.

"That was easy," Heidi says.

"Odd." A handwritten letter catches Molly's eye. She picks it up and reads, "January 12, 1922. We regret to inform you of the passing of Mina's mother from influenza last Tuesday. Although it is customary for such children to be sent to an orphanage, I trust that, with your connections, you might be able to find her an apprenticeship so she may be cared for." She turns the letter over, "It's unsigned."

"Let's find Hillary." Heidi nudges her mother who is deep in thought.

They walk back down the long corridor and Molly chooses a key at random and tries it in the lock. She tries another, then another and on her fourth try, the deadbolt slips out with a clunk.

As I watch the group interact with the Guardians, I travel through time back to my ten-year old self who is still alive. Lying on the treatment table, leather straps tethering her to her fate, she's numbed by fear, abandonment and anger, but she's alive nonetheless, and I wonder if there is such a thing as resolution. If it is true that we choose our own journey within an all-powerful previously decided life course, then what have I chosen?

I chose to believe in my fates as they occurred, I chose to stay the course of life, but within that, I chose a focus that led me down a dark path. Even though I was born with light within me, I allowed each encounter with darkness to chisel away at my soul until darkness took over. I suppose if I'm honest, I chose that too.

As I sit with my completed cycle of rage, visiting those past events, sending that fury from one person from the past to another, I feel no sense of completion. For eons I've longed to retrieve those lost parts of me, which I believe I'd left with the people of my past—the Unibrow, the druids, the mean boy, my mother. But, all I'd managed to finish was a completion of a never-ending circuit of rage, which continues despite my desire to pass it to those who hurt me most during my life. If only I could give them back the pain and grief they laid on me so long ago. But that day never comes and the pain continues and more people suffer in the wake of my fury.

I realize that if I do not stop this circuit, I will soon cease to exist. It feels like I am dangerously close to non-existence.

Where is the justice? For all the years of torture, of pain, of imprisonment (false and otherwise), a piece of my soul desires justice. Is that so wrong? From my perch between lives, I sit waiting for the arms of the cosmic timepiece to fall into rhythm with the planets. I long for the solution, resolution and final decision to settle into my soul's core and finally release this relentless hatred and ire that has been stored in me through thousands of lifetimes and millions of years.

Thus far, my choice has been to gather Hillary, Heidi and Molly's gifts in order to consume them and free myself. But what occurred was beyond my comprehension, my scope of knowledge granted me a dim limited view of what was truly possible in my life.

Regardless, I'm so close to non-existence, it doesn't seem to matter what choice I make. It appears that I am on a path to nothingness.

From the looks of it, I have two options. Live a few more millennia with the help of the women's extrasensory gifts doing...what? Perpetuating the cycle of masterfully obtaining then consuming other's treasures?

Then there is nothingness. Would it be so bad to not be here? My energetic constructs would most likely be either recycled or reabsorbed into Source energy. The universe would likely be better without me anyway.

As I watch the group make their way down the hall, I see that they should be allowed to discover my past. It couldn't possibly do any harm to permit them to see what a mess can be made with a single lifetime.

I give them my unspoken blessing as I watch them open the door to the acupuncture treatment room. My body looks so small on the enormous table with the thick leather restrains and metal buckles rubbing my smooth skin raw. This was one thing, in all my lifetimes that I was unable to fix.

There are so many other things I would have done differently, but my experience in this room is an exception. What can one do when one is forced to stay, tethered to a painful outcome?

Yes, non-existence is a mere breath away. One more sigh, a simple inhale and exhale and I will dissolve into nothingness. My inhale comes easily. Smooth. Clear. Simple. "What a pleasure it could have been to exist on Earth" and I remember my father as I disappear into my exhale.

CHAPTER XVII

Stealth Guardian

Ritual: Father Truth
Element: Silver
Planet: Mercury

Sit in front of a mirror and say the following:
The truth comes from within me and I see it clearly.

Repeat for seven days consecutively. If you miss a day, you must start again.

When you are finished, know that your truth is what matters. Others may have their own truths and no one truth can replace another.

On the eighth day of this ritual sit in front of the mirror and say:
I am whole. I am beautiful.

Molly hesitates, her hand ready to turn the key to the treatment room. "I'm afraid of what we'll find."

"Come on, Mom. You know we have to," says Heidi.

Molly nods, and her hand slowly turns the weathered, chipped brass doorknob and she slowly opens the heavy wood door. The door's creak echoes down the hallway and Molly and Heidi step into the stuffy treatment room. The only light comes from the gas street lamps from through the barred window.

Molly gasps at the sight of Mina's little body strapped to the treatment table. Needles protrude from her forehead, her arms, her abdomen and her feet. Molly gingerly places her hand on the girl's neck to check for a pulse. "She's alive, but barely. Help me unbuckle her."

"Aunt Hillary. Can you hear us?" Heidi's voice trembles as she helps her mother release the restraints.

"Who on earth would do this to a child?" Molly carefully begins to remove the needles and says to Heidi, "Sweetie, will you look around for some water? I'm sure she needs some."

"The girl can't be more than my age." Heidi heads out the door to look for water.

She finds a basin with a full pitcher of water and a mug in the office and she brings it back to the treatment room. By now, Molly has removed all the needles and is gently massaging the girl's arms and legs. "Can you hear us?"

"It's hard to believe Aunt Hillary is in there." Heidi pours water into the mug then walks over to peer into Mina's wan face.

"Well," Molly quietly brushes a few wayward strands of hair from Mina's cheek, "None of us really looks like herself right now, do we?" She glances over into the mirror at the reflection of Krystal Sykes.

Molly looks at Heidi. "I think we can carry her. Can you get her legs and I'll grab her shoulders."

Mina's body is surprisingly light and Molly chokes up at the thought of someone leaving a child like this. They carry her out into the hallway and walk back toward the Iron Shinto, carefully stepping inside the room and gently laying Mina on the stone floor.

"Think we can get back to Moa and the airplane with this contraption? I'm not sure how to make it take off or lift off or whatever it does." Molly calls out, "Guardian! Hello! We need you!"

Heidi begins to laugh, "You don't have to shout, Mommy. The Guardians are right here and can hear you just fine."

"Oh." Molly chuckles too. "Can we go back to Moa now?"

"Not yet," Heidi says. "The Guradian wants you to promise to love yourself as you would love me."

"But I don't know the Guardian. How could I love him?"

"Not the Guardian, mom." Heidi says sweetly. "Love yourself like you love me." pointing to herself.

Molly takes a minute, then shrugs. "Okay. I guess I can do that."

"No." Heidi says. "The Guardian doesn't believe you."

"Well, what's is going to take? We need to get back to Moa." Molly is annoyed now.

Heidi doesn't say anything. The group stands in the Iron Shinto on the verge of reuniting their bodies and their Ka and yet, something is missing.

"Well." Molly, out of patience, raises her voice. "What does he say?"

"He's not saying anything," Heidi whispers.

"Why are you whispering?" Molly speaks in her normal voice. "I'm through with these games." She projects her voice outward to the unseen Guardians. "Okay Guardians. You brought us here now take us back to Moa so we can reunite with our bodies."

"I'm whispering because we're in the presence of the all-knowing, all-seeing universal power. Some call it God, Buddha, Allah, Source." Heidi bows her head and sits quietly.

"Where?" Molly looks through the Iron Shinto's window, then through the door searching for this new presence.

"It's not out there," Heidi says in a quiet voice. "It's in here." Heidi puts her hand on her mother's heart.

Molly is speechless.

"There is a reason our bodies separated from our Ka so easily. The Guardian wants you to tell him why you abandoned yourself," Heidi says solemnly.

As Molly searches for the words to explain, Mina's body, which has up to this point been motionless on the Iron Shinto's floor, begins to emanate light. It's as if her insides are glowing and light is escaping through her eyelids, her fingernails, ears and hair.

"I…" Molly begins to shake then does her best to calm herself before she speaks. "As a soul, I decided to come into my body and this family for a reason. There were certain lessons I wished to work on and I agreed to the events, moving to Hawaii, having Heidi and even accepting Steve's death. But as my soul entered my body, someone or something cut off my life essence. It was as if they grabbed my air supply hose and bent it so I could no longer breathe. They told me the agreement had changed. The entity said my life would be a preordained set of events which were different from the ones that I'd chosen before. If I refused, I would die."

160

Molly's words come out in chokes sobs. "I agreed, but only because I didn't want to die. I wanted Heidi and even though I would lose Steve at a young age, I wanted to have the time with him. That's why I agreed. I don't know how I could have done things differently…"

"You couldn't…" Mina is now up and alert. Her skin is luminous. "I understand because I, too, was forced to agree to a life contract which was different from the one I had chosen. It made me bitter and ugly."

"Hillary?" Molly is shocked.

"No. I have allowed Hillary's Ka to return to her body. She is safe with Moa." Mina looks at the group now. "I apologize. Please forgive me and understand that I was the one who trapped you. It was all designed to force you to work together so that I could take your gifts, your group gifts, as a way to consume them. It was wrong, I know. But your words, the ones that set you apart are your truth, Molly. What they did was show me that was wrong."

"What do you mean 'group gifts?" Heidi asks shyly.

"I don't have much time but I can explain before I go." Mina smiles at Heidi. "When souls enter into a physical body and choose a family there is a rare thing that can happen. Beyond the genetic connection, the souls can make a pact, which supersedes any karmic, earthly contract. You three have such a contract and I wished to break it apart for my own purposes.

"What stopped you?" Molly asks.

"Your experience with the forceful interjection of that entity before your birth," Mina says. "When I heard you speak of it, I understood something vital in my own personal growth. We are from the same soul group. I did not recognize you because I was long blinded to the good in life and to those people who could support me. I knew you could help me, but up until a few minutes ago, I didn't know why. Now, I must go. I have expended the last of my energy to communicate with your group."

"Where are you going?" Heidi asks.

"To non-existence." The light emanating from inside Mina dims slightly. "I am an advanced soul who used her time on earth unwisely and has moved beyond the scope of our soul group's work. There is a limit to the achievement of an advanced soul. As we move up, the work we do becomes more challenging and time constraints are a part of the work. My time was up before I concluded my work and therefore I must go."

"That doesn't seem fair." Heidi says.

"Heidi, sweetie." Molly puts her hand on her daughter's shoulder. "There's compassion and then there is softness. How do we even know that Hillary's Ka is back in her body? How do we know that this isn't a trick?"

"You're right, Molly." Mina nods, her light dimming slightly. "I can only speak my truth but I cannot make you believe or understand. Faith is the only thing that connects me to my truth. If that is lost, then I am lost." After a moment, Mina lifts her skirt to expose her right ankle, "This tattoo is a good example of just that. When I arrived on this earth, I was, as you can imagine, horrified that I'd given up my right to choose the life I wanted. It is, in fact, a human's most basic right of existence. So upset was I that I began to leave my body, disappear for hours at a time. Oh, my body would be there, but my soul was elsewhere. One day I was shocked to see that a group of indigenous Japanese, or Ainu had marked me with a tribal symbol. I had absolutely no choice in the matter."

"Couldn't you have run away?" Heidi is rapt.

"Yes, I could have run as far as the hills, to the shores of the ocean or even taken a boat away into the sea. But, you see, I still was there. The lack of commitment of really being here on earth made it easy for negative or even horrifying experiences to happen to me. The more I saw those negative things happen, the more I was convinced that I was doomed to failure and not just in this life, but in all lives. It was then that I decided to do the bare minimum. I split my 'self,' my focus and my Ka in half. I was on earth enough to exist, but I was really somewhere else. Every part of me desired to be off this earth and that is when I tried to end my life." Mina reveals the inside scars on her wrists.

The entire group recoils in horror.

"Of course, the acupuncturist would have none of that. Not on his watch, at least. He saved my life and placed me in confinement. He reasoned it was for my own safety. I did not know that my mother had died. I learned of her fate as you read the letter, Molly." Mina's light is almost out. "Again, all my senses were blocked by my own belief that the soul's journey from body to the energetic realm was worthless. Why, bother if there is no choice."

Molly begins to weep softly, "That's how I felt."

As the last of Mina's emanating light disappears she manages, "Yes. I know. Please forgive me my transgressions. We are, after all, family." Mina's body disintegrates before their eyes.

It's as if she was never there. The group sits in stunned silence until, suddenly, the Iron Shinto's door begins to close.

CHAPTER XVIII

Surrender

Ritual: Healing Psychic Injury
Element: Copper
Planet: Mars

*Pick a flower with petals (any kind you wish) and stand before a
body of running water (creek, stream, river).
Drop each petal into the running water as you say:
I forgive myself and release the past.
When you have released all the petals and hold the stem and
leaves say the following:
The source of my pain no longer lives within me.
Throw the entire stem and leaves into the running water.*

Repeat as necessary.

Psychic pain is beyond anything I've ever experienced. In physical pain, one can seek help from the physical world; in psychic pain, one can only heal oneself. As I pass through the membrane of consciousness into the realm of non-existence, my soul experiences a psychic pain so intense, my soul is taken over by darkness, my soul energy flicks off and I finally forgive the one person who I have blamed all along for my lifetimes of misfortune. I forgive myself and succumb to the nothingness with an ease I've never before experienced. I finally realize that the one person I had to answer to all along has been me and once I do that, I am complete.

CHAPTER XIX

Soul Credit

Ritual: Soul Space
Element: Gold
Star: Sun

Perform the Sacred Space Ritual before this one. While in your sacred space, imagine you are light. Now, turn up the brightness of this light so that it encompasses your entire being. Then imagine you float beyond your sacred space to a new place. This one is beyond your self, beyond your world and it is your place of origin. This is your soul space.
Within your soul space, you can find support, love and healing beyond the confines of a physical body.

As you sit in your soul space, what do you see, feel, taste, smell and hear? Allow whatever healing or information that needs to come in to do so.

When you are ready, come back into your body. Allow yourself some time to ground and center with your new knowledge and healing.

The Iron Shinto door opens to reveal the threshold of Moa's airplane. Now, there is no question of its existence and the Molly dashes forward with Heidi and the rest of the group at her heels.

There, seated next to Moa, is Hillary.

"Hold on Molly!" Moa puts her hand up and smiles. "We've got a little work to do."

With a wave of her hand, Moa manifests a magical glimmering pool that stretches the width of the plane and takes up the space between the group and Hillary and Moa.

"Jump in!" Hillary laughs. "The water is great!"

The two Heidi's look at each other and do a cannon ball creating a huge splash. With a squeal, each of them reunites with their own ka.

Molly is next and she and her body dive in head-first reemerging as fully integrated souls and bodies.

Krystal, now herself again, looks around in wonderment at her new surroundings, "What the…"

Hillary helps Krystal and Molly out of the pool as Moa sends out a beam of light that surrounds the security guard and Adem's carrier and lifts them over the water. Because neither can swim, Moa uses extra care. Each is carefully dipped into the pool with a strong beam of energy supporting their weight.

Then Moa gently sets the carrier down and nods to the security guard, the teenager and Krystal. "Thank you for your help. You may go home now." With a wave of Moa's hand, she sends a beautiful energy light, which sends Krystal, the teenager and the security guard back home to Los Tardos.

Suddenly, a flash of light blinds Molly and Hillary and when their eyes adjust, Adem is gone!

"Where did he go?" Hillary yells.

"Maybe he went into the pool." Molly screams and jumps in the pool as does Hillary and Heidi.

After resurfacing, Molly begins to scream, "Adem! Adem!"

Another blinding flash of light and the plane disappears. The group floats in the middle of a light field and Molly cries into the light, "You cannot do this to me! I will not allow another person to be taken from me."

All is silent. Then a booming male voices says, "Are you going to let them kick you for the rest of your life?"

A light tunnel opens up above the group and they are all sucked upward into a river of light. It is at once calming and exhilarating. They are surrounded by a gentle hum and whoosh as if they are traveling through time, space and dimensions.

Each individual has her own experience, yet the group moves as one in the same direction.

Molly, the most upset of the group understands at once. They are moving toward Source! Her emotions calm as she is swept up through this portal and into the warmest welcome she's ever received. It's as if the light nestles into her heart and shows her where home is within herself.

Hillary, however, resists the peace and comfort surrounding her. She squirms and wiggles remembering all the negative unfinished business left in her world. In particular, the Crone/Mina and all the harm she's caused. After all, the group followed Ku's story in horror as he struggled through his life without his precious healing gifts. Why should she embrace the light when there is still so much darkness in the world?

The group is reassembled in a light chamber. Two tall pillar-like beings stand before them and the group is engulfed in light from the inside out.

Heidi smiles at her mom, "You look like a light bulb."

"This is most unusual." The first being speaks in a low rumbling voice. "Our intervention comes at a time when most of your earth lives are still incomplete."

Hillary figures these are judges from heaven and her thoughts are answered by the first being. "You are incorrect, Hillary. Our souls have progressed closer to Source but we are not here to judge. Our presence is merely to guide you on your chosen life path. Because your soul group is so advanced, meaning you've had millennia after millennia of lifetimes on many planets including Earth, you require less intervention than the average soul. Your group consists of those who are in various states of incarnation from currently occupying an Earth body to spirit Guides who have left the earthly realm. This range gives your group a unique richness and unparalleled ability to complete karma."

The middle being has a melodic voice and seems to sing the words, "If we had not intervened, you all would have shifted with Mina into non-existence. In other words, your souls would cease to exist."

Gasps and comments run through the group.

"But I thought we had a choice?" Hillary says.

"Your path has taken an uncharted turn due to the choice of one of your members." The first being booms. "She has chosen non-existence over allowing her actions to play out in the usual karmic fashion of cause and effect. With her actions, she has stopped the negative effects of her most heinous acts, however, in doing so, she has rendered your entire soul group's work null and void."

"What exactly does that mean?" Hillary asks.

"In order to save your souls from total obliteration, you must complete Mina's karmic lineage." The first being rumbles. "In your soul group, you are minus one."

"Who are we missing?" Heidi asks.

"The one of you who has suffered the most and chosen the path of soul annihilation. Mina," the second being says.

"Mina? One of us?" Hillary shrieks.

"She's one of them, too!" Heidi points to the large beings.

Hillary shakes her head. "I think you're mistaken. She has been trying to imprison us and steal our gifts. She stole Ku's gifts. She is EVIL!"

"We are all connected, Hillary," he first being says. "When one suffers we all suffer and when one celebrates we all do as well. When Mina chose this to be her last incarnation, she left one final piece of karma undone."

"Why should we help her?" Hillary scoffs. "I was trapped in her body and nearly didn't escape."

"How do you think you did escape?" the second being asks.

Hillary throws the second being a puzzled look but the first being continues.

"We offer you this piece of advice before you choose. And you do have a choice in this matter." The first being's voice resonates so loudly, waves of sound ripple through the group's energy. "What is your common bond? Think back through each of your lives and what is it that you all have sought, above all else."

"I haven't 'sought' a thing." Hillary laughs. "I was just here for the ride."

"If you wish to believe that," the first being says, "that will be your truth. But what if you did have a common bond beyond your earthly desire for love and attention? What if there was more to your connection than mere childhood spats and games?"

Hillary bristles, "I don't like the way this conversation is going. Mina intended to cause my family and me great harm!"

"True," the first voice rumbles. "And what skills would you lack if you did not have those experiences?"

Hillary takes a moment. "Why are you asking me? She inflicted the harm on me, Molly and Heidi."

"Because," the second being intones, "you must take responsibility."

"For what?" Hillary is upset. "She almost killed us. She was cruel and hateful and she trapped us in the Iron Shinto and then me in her own body!"

"Are you going to let her continue to hurt you? Hillary, you have the power to think thoughts that can stop your past from replaying in your mind," the first being says. "You can either perpetuate the cycle of abuse again and again with your thoughts or you can heal them by seeking learning. That is the fastest, most direct path out of abuse."

Neither being speaks and Hillary senses a building pressure around her. "Okay. Compassion, I learned compassion while I was in Mina's body. Self-reliance. I learned to speak up, too..."

"Stop right there," The first being says. "All of you. Think back to one of the most challenging events in your life. Is it possible that you share a common learning path?"

"After Steve passed away," Molly says, "I had to speak up and learn to do things on my own."

Molly's statement is greeted with approval from the group.

"Me too!" Heidi finally speaks up. "I held my feelings inside after Daddy died and was afraid to cry or say I was hurt."

"Mina's lineage, including her previous incarnation, Minamoto Yoritomo, receded into non-existence with her," the second being says. "When karma goes unfinished, it is passed down the lineage. Since there is no lineage, the karma has now been passed to you. Your soul group is responsible for completing Mina's karma. In her case the unfinished piece is to retrieve the inner voice."

"But whose inner voice?" Molly asks. "Haven't we all learned to speak up in one way or another in our lives?"

"You did, but Mina didn't" the first being says. "Therefore, you have not completed your soul group's task."

"As we said, you do have a choice." The first being is speaking. "You may finish out the task we've laid out for your group to complete Mina's karma or begin your soul's journey again. This is a group decision."

"What does it mean to begin our soul's journey again?" Heidi asks tentatively.

"Your soul's memory and learning, vibrational existence and uniqueness will be wiped clean and your millennia of lifetimes in Universe after Universe will be gone. You will begin again, just as any soul who is born must do."

"I don't know about you guys, but I certainly don't want to start my soul's journey all over again," Hillary says valiantly. "What do you think?"

Molly looks at Heidi who nods in assent, "Let's do it."

"We will leave it to you to find the inner voice." The first being's voice vibrates with such force, that the group bounces as if on a giant trampoline of clouds.

"But," Molly sputters. "The only person who has that information is Mina and she is no longer here!"

"You all have the ability to find the inner voice if you work together," the first being says. "The information is within each of you and by sharing your knowledge with one another, Minamoto's inner voice will be found. When you retrieve it, you will have completed your soul group's task. Remember, it is within your power."

A blinding light zaps each individual and they slip and slide back down a light tunnel and land with a gentle thump in the airplane.

"Adem!" Molly finds the infant sleeping peacefully in his carrier wedged between two seats.

Heidi looks around. "Mom, where are we?"

"Back on Moa's plane, but beyond that," Molly picks Adem up, cradles him and sniffs his head, "I have no idea."

"We're in Japan," Moa says. "Time to put our heads together and find the inner voice."

"Isn't an inner voice intangible?" Hillary asks.

"Not necessarily," Moa says. "The light guardians said we all had the answers and if we worked together we would find it."

"I don't even know where to start." Molly strokes Adem's head and kisses his head.

"Let's go over what we do know about Mina and her experiences on Earth that led her to her decision to cease to exist."

"She certainly chose a dark path." Hillary groans.

"True." Moa says. "Mina also had a great amount of suffering as a young child. In fact, she ended up separating from her body because of that suffering."

"While I was trapped in Mina's body, I definitely felt pain—both mental and physical. When she released me, I kept being drawn to the Iron Shinto."

"When we found the Iron Shinto, she appeared there, as well," Molly adds.

"Perhaps that is the best place to start."

"Sounds as good a place as any other," Hillary says.

"Since we're all in our own bodies," Moa smiles, "we don't need the plane anymore."

"I don't know," Molly says hesitantly. "Last time we traveled this way, we got stuck."

"Trust me," Moa says, "We are safe." Then with a wave of her hand, "To the Iron Shinto!"

The group dissolves into shimmering light. However, Moa feels a magnetic pull away from their destination.

"Oh, no!" Moa uses her powers to create a safety container around Molly, Heidi and Hillary to protect their reentry. However, where they will reenter Earth is anybody's guess.

CHAPTER XX

Disillusion Resolution

Ritual: Soul Group Guidance
Element: Gold
Star: Sun

This ritual builds on the Sacred Space Ritual and the Soul Space Ritual. After performing each of these rituals you are ready to perform the Soul Group Guidance Ritual.

In your Soul Space you may encounter other souls who are made of light. This is your soul group. These souls are your fans, your friends and your deepest admirers. They are beyond your family for they have been your family for many, many incarnations.

As with the Soul Space ritual, you may experience healing or new information that was not possible within the confines of your body. You may also notice other light beings around you and you may ask their names and communicate with them. They may have stories to

tell you or they may simply send you love. Receive whatever learning
or emotions they have to give and know that you are in a profound
space which you may revisit any time you wish.

Moa has done her best to create a protective container for each person in the group, but her powers are no match for the intense magnetic pull.

With a jolt, the group reanimates into the Iron Shinto, which the King has placed in the Egyptian stone dungeon at the exact moment when Mina, as the Crone, buries her hand in Ku's chest and steals his healing gifts.

Horrified, Heidi begins to cry and runs to comfort Ku, who cannot see, feel or hear her.

"Oh, Mom. What do we do?" Heidi says tearfully as her hands pass right through Ku's body.

Luckily, Heidi can receive an embrace from her mother. Molly holds her daughter and does her best not to cry as well.

"Why are we here?" Hillary tries to stay calm after witnessing the frightening event. "Okay. Poor Ku looks so distraught. Surely there is a way to heal what he was not able to do in this moment."

Molly manages to contain her emotions enough to speak. "We can't undo the damage Mina has already done."

"Right," Heidi says. "Moa. You should have a better idea of what we need to do."

"I have just about as much information and insight as the rest of you. The beings were right. We must work together." Moa is silent, then says, "If this is about the inner voice, what is it that Mina could not say?"

"Sorry I took your gifts and destroyed your life?" Hillary says sarcastically.

Molly has a faraway look on her face and seems to speak from that place. "I'm sorry. I was only perpetuating the pattern of abuse set out before me."

"Mom!" Heidi shouts. But, Molly cannot answer.

"Your mom is channeling Mina right now, sweetie." Hillary puts her arm around Heidi and they are amazed at what Molly says next.

"My belief that my life and direction was hopeless led me down a path which created a place of no alternative. When I look at myself then, I remember so vividly how cruel I thought life was. I was so upset at what life was doing to me and yet I was doing it to myself. Each time I had a choice even if it didn't look like I had one. The choice came after in not perpetuating the abuse. For example, the boy. He kicked me one time but I kicked me thousands of times.

Molly continues to channel Mina, "I am so sorry. So, so sorry. If I could take it back I would. But I would say, "If something bad happens to you, let that be the end of it. Make a vow to continue on your life, not as you were, but as a newly transformed being with a strengthened resolve and belief that you are not alone. That there is a power greater than you and that you can trust yourself to be yourself, not despite but inclusive of your tragedies."

By now Moa, Hillary, and Heidi are listening intently, eyes wide. "Life has many tragedies. Some great and some small. Each one is unique and offers learning with its experience. After the learning, we can use that event to fuel our hatred for ourselves and others, or we can use that learning to fuel our love for ourselves and others.

Which will it be? Which will you perpetuate?"

The women watch in amazement as a pus-filled, roiling blob appears before them, morphs into the Crone and then back into little Mina.

As little Mina appears, the group dissolves into light and Moa does her best, once again, to set up protection for Hillary, Heidi and Molly. "Hang on, I think we will be taken to a few of these scenes until we complete the necessary resolutions. Then, I think, we'll be allowed to use the Iron Shinto for travel. If my hunch is right, we will be able to use the Iron Shinto to get you back home."

Moa is right, the group reappears and this time, they are standing in a large room with a glowing fireplace. In it sits an obese woman about forty years old with a caterpillar-like unibrow. She is alone at a desk and appears to be poured into a wooden chair, her girth spilling over the sides. Her quill makes scratching noises as she mumbles and speaks to herself.

"Pardon." Hillary tries to touch the woman's shoulder but, just as Heidi experienced with Ku, her hand goes right through. This woman cannot see, hear or feel them either.

"Anyone get anything from this scene?" Molly asks.

"I hear children laughing," Heidi says. "They are playing a game." She pauses trying to decipher what she is hearing then says, "It's some kind of song. I can't understand the words, though."

"I see Mina stealing this little girl's gifts as well." Hillary says. "But, she seems perfectly content in her negative world."

"Then why are we here?" Molly asks.

"I think we need to let Mina speak once again," Moa says. "I think I know what this is about." She nods to herself then laughs, "Okay, okay. I got it." Moa grabs Molly's and Hillary's hands and begins to sing, "Wa-ter. The Wa-ter. Mina for-got the wa-ter."

Molly takes hold of Hillary's and Heidi's hands, and the group skips around in a circle singing and laughing. By the third round of singing, the enormous woman with the unibrow slips out of her chair and begins to dance, too. With a look of ecstasy on her face, the woman begins to twirl and sing and eventually, she opens the door and skips outside.

The room dissolves and the group is left in light.

"I hear a woman singing," Heidi says brightly.

"Yes," Hillary says. "I can see her giving a little girl a bath."

Moa shakes her head. "This can't be right. I'm getting that this woman had her gifts stolen when she was four years old."

Molly reflexively puts her hand over her chest. "I feel such love and grace coming from this woman. Her beauty radiates from her soul and her child has the same thing."

"This love and grace that she has created throughout her life has placed a protective sphere around her and her child."

"Amazing!" Molly says.

"What could Mina possibly have to say to her?" Hillary asks.

The group watches as the woman cups the water in her hands and lets it gently roll down her child's body. Then she picks up a cloth and pats the little girl dry. Wrapping her up, the woman takes the little girl in her arms and says, "Forgiveness gives us the grace to create whatever our heart desires. It is from this place that no one can harm us or cause us pain. It is from grace that we grow closer to Source. Thank you, Mina. And thank you to the woman and little girls who surround us now. You are the witness to the miracle of creation. From this creation, anything is possible."

A stunning light envelops the group and they are shrunk to the size of acorns and find themselves inside a tree trunk. Five wee druids are lined up as a filmy large mass floats around them.

The druids chant, "Oh, Great Witch. We worship your work, your wealth, your craft."

Unbeknownst to the druids, the filmy substance is spiritually picking their pockets, cleaning out not only their precious gifts, but also their hard-earned positive energy flow and happiness.

"These people are worshiping a vampire but they don't know it?" Heidi says.

One of the druids stands and removes her hood. It's Mina!

"Mina," Heidi runs up to her, "please, hear me! This woman has created a false place for you to heal. You're fine the way you are! You are fine the way you are!"

The Great Witch's filmy form turns a murky gray, then falls to the earth. As the druid ritual continues, the facilitator grabs a broom and ceremonially sweeps the Great Witch right out of a knot hole entrance where she is transformed by the sun into earth energy—recycling along with the leaves and roots, feeding the earth.

Heidi, Molly, Hillary and Moa walk out the knothole and into the forest, and they are sucked into an earthen tunnel slide. Down, down, down they go, protected by a light tube, they travel through the molten center of Earth and on into absolute darkness. Suddenly, the Earth spits them out onto a freshly plowed field.

Dusting herself off, Hillary is the first to speak. "Where are we now?"

"I can only imagine after what we've been through," Molly says.

In the distance is a tiny house with a few trees around and a rock path leading up the front entrance.

Heading toward the house, Hillary says, "I have a sinking feeling about this."

Her fears are answered with an unearthly howl coming from within the walls of the house.

"On second thought..." Hillary begins to step away.

"If we don't finish this job, we're dead anyway." Molly's tone is ominous.

"That's not what the Guardians said," Hillary counters.

"I know," Molly says. "But I 'know' that this is it for us, as well as Mina, if we do not find the inner voice."

With a deep breath, Hillary takes a step toward the house and another howl stops her in her tracks. But after another breath, Hillary walks up the steps with Moa, Heidi and Molly in tow. Inside, the house is musty and dark, but as they round the corner into a bedroom, they see a witch doctor. His gnome-like figure is clothed in a red robe, which is tied with a wide gold brocade sash. The gold paint on his ceremonial mask catches the last bit of setting sun and he carries an animal skin cinched at the top.

Again, the girls cannot be seen or heard. But Molly approaches anyway, fascinated by what she is witnessing. The witch doctor begins to ring bells and chant in an ancient language.

Mina's weary little body lies on the bed below him.

"Funny," Molly says. "Mina 'feels' different to me than the previous times I've experienced her."

As the witch doctor raises his hands to begin a sweep over Mina's body, Hillary says, "She has armor. We've got to stop him. She has a protective armor and he is about to sweep it off!"

The witch doctor continues with his ritual and, much to the upset of the group, no one is able to stop him.

Molly is close to tears. "Oh, I can't take it any more. This man swept all of Mina's protection from her. This is where her trouble began. What can we possibly say to heal this awful circumstance?"

Moa who has been quiet for quite some time, finally speaks. "It is not ours to stop. It is ours to heal. By witnessing her pain, we reveal its existence."

The house explodes, scattering the group in opposite directions, however, they land in the same location. They are in the hallway of the acupuncturist's office with the Iron Shinto.

"I recognize this place," Heidi says.

"Perhaps we need to retrieve another part of Mina," Molly says. "Odd that we would need to do this all over again."

Molly puts her hand on the doorknob and slowly opens the door. Inside, the acupuncturist is placing needles into Mina's little arm. "…no pain no gain," are his final words to her.

"We allow pain into our lives in order to heal those parts of us we wish to grow," Hillary says as they all look upon the sad scene. "I felt what it was like to be trapped inside her body and it was one of the most terrifying experiences of my life. Mina, whatever happened to you, I hope you know we now understand." Hillary begins to cry softly at the memory this scene brings up.

The acupuncturist cries out as he is suddenly flung to the floor by an invisible force. Needles float from a cabinet over to his body and plunge in a seemingly random pattern into the insides of both of his arms.

"What is happening?" Hillary asks in alarm.

"Looks like Mina has somehow reemerged from her non-existence and is seeking revenge. It could be someone or something else at work, I'm not sure."

"I think we have our answer," Heidi says wanly pointing to the acupuncturist's arms.

The group is shocked to see the words "No pain" on one arm and "No Gain" on the other.

Suddenly, the group is frozen in place. No one can move and the fiery glow of Mina hovers near the ceiling. "Thank you for restoring my energy, group. I now am able to complete my final task—sending the Royal Family of Jupiter into non-existence."

"But, we helped you heal!" Hillary says.

"I heard what you said outside my house just before you encountered the witch doctor." Mina's fire crackles with her voice, "You did this for yourselves. If your lives were not in danger, you would have left me and my life to rot."

"Maybe so," Hillary says, "but look at yourself. Why on earth would we help you? You've inflicted harm upon us at every turn." Then she's hit with a profound revelation. "I've been storing your negativity for you while you regained your energy! You were using me to perpetuate your own hatred!"

Just then, Hillary realizes what she needs to do. There is a reason why Mina was so eager to get their group gift. It has power, most likely more power than Mina has, and as Hillary looks to Heidi, Molly and Moa, they smile at her. Suddenly she knows how to stop Mina at her own game.

With a knowing nod to Hillary, Molly whispers to the group. "What are we focusing on?"

"Why not try the truth?" Hillary asks loudly, staring directly as Mina.

Mina shoots a stream of fire at them, snapping and popping, sending energetic embers dangerously close to the group. "Try your best. It won't work."

Hillary wonders what the truth looks like and decides to see the word written across Mina's chest.

Heidi sends tinkling bells ringing a song of truth into Mina's soul.

Molly feels the triumph of her first experience of truth when she had said goodbye to her beloved husband, Steve.

And Moa surrounds herself with truth and gives it to Mina as a gift.

The result astounds even Mina. The flames dissipate and Mina floats to the floor. The acupuncturist is released from his restraints and he scurries from the room and the entire room becomes the Iron Shinto.

"I can't go," Mina says, tears streaming down her already wet face. "She's not here."

"Yes," the voice shows up before the woman, then the tang of ginger permeates the air. "I'm here my love. You're home now." Mina's mother walks through a misty light and Mina runs to her, embracing her with a lifetime of sadness and love. She and her mother are luminous. Their light energy intermingles the hues of destiny, heartbreak and warmth all rolled up together. The result surrounds the pair with a gorgeous color wheel pulsing with love.

"And now to complete my goal." Mina takes her mother's hand and leads her toward the Iron Shinto, but as Mina steps over the threshold, the Shinto vanishes. That which she has worked so hard for—finding her family's inner voice—has disintegrated within an instant.

Crestfallen, Mina addresses the group. "I have failed once again to obtain my genealogical inner voice. It was encased in an iron ball and placed within the walls of the Iron Shinto." She softly weeps, her head lowered. "Perhaps," she continues tearily, "my destiny is to stay with my mother and accept that my lineage is incompl…"

Mina is interrupted by the sound of a man clearing his throat. As she whirls around, she comes face to face with the King of Jupiter. In his outstretched hand is the iron ball, which contains Mina's family's inner voice. "I have been waiting to give this to you for a very, very long time, Mina. Please accept this with the honor only a King may bestow upon another royal entity."

Taking the ball in both hands, Mina bows deeply to the King. "Thank you. Your challenges brought me to where and who I am right now. For that I will be forever grateful."

The King steps back as Mina holds the ball, unsure of what to do next. The ball begins to vibrate and cracks open revealing a blindingly beautiful bright blue light. As a dense cylinder of blue light penetrates Mina's throat, then her mother's, a line of relatives appears behind her and Minamoto Yoritomo appears, front and center, at the start of the line. Like a string of pearls, the light sends its thick, vibrant ray, which connects each individual. Thousands of people, aged and youthful, rested and weary have shown up to receive the family's birthright of an inner voice.

A filmy mist floats down from above, pools next to Mina and finally takes the form of Mina's father. His wiry beard and flyaway mane are exactly as she remembered them. Respectfully bowing his head, he says proudly, "Well done, Mina."

She rushes to her father and gives him a firm hug. Inhaling his familiar earthy scent, Mina tucks her head into his chest the way she used to, long ago. Fractals of blue, green and indigo light bounce off of the two as they embrace. Waves of color pour out from them, the love energy pulsating with yellow and pink.

As Moa, Molly, Heidi and Hillary take in the miraculous scene, Hillary says, "Well, I guess it's time we all go back home."

With tears welling in her eyes, Molly's eyes move to someone right behind Hillary. It's the old woman from Hillary's flight to Los Tardos!

Confused, Hillary says wryly, "Couldn't get enough of me on the plane, eh? What unfinished business could I possibly have with you?"

Molly embraces her sister and gently whispers into her ear, "Listen to my words as if they are beams of love."

Hillary pulls back from her sister and searches her face. Molly's eyes are spilling over with tears and with love, and

Hillary begins to tremble all over. Drawing her close again, Molly whispers, "Shh..shh…" Molly is rocking Hillary gently. "Sweetie, your plane never made it to Los Tardos."

Hillary shrieks in horror. "What?? No!!" She pulls away from her sister, shaking her head. "No, that's not possible. That's crazy! Stop saying things like that?

The old woman comes to stand next to Hillary and places a soft hand on her back, and Hillary starts to whimper, but no tears appear.

Molly continues. "You went down in the Pacific, Hil. It all happened very fast."

Images flash through Hillary's mind, of the suffocating tunnel that turned out to be a blanket, the alabaster and blood red pus oozing blob which was actually the pale skin and red lipstick of the flight attendant. Maybe this was a trick? "But…the cart hit my arm and it hurt. The clear air turbulence…we made it through okay."

"No, Sweetie, you didn't" Molly nods toward the kindly old woman. "Violet here was your Transition Guide."

Hillary looks at the woman and feels a sense of peace and calm come over her.

Molly says, "I wondered when I saw you sitting with Moa on her invisible plane, then I figured it out during our journey before we healed Mina, and the light pillar beings confirmed your passage telepathically with me."

Hillary shakes her head again. "Wow. I don't know what to think." She looks at her hands, turning them over, furrowing her brow.

Molly wraps her arms around her sister, holds her tight as a sob escapes. "Oh, Hil. I love you so much, but you know what I learned? No one really ever dies. We outgrow our bodies. Because we are in the same soul group, our souls live on and, no matter what form we are in or what stage of incarnation, we will always be together."

Hillary manages to speak after taking a few gulps of air, "Oh, the irony. Looks like my hypnotherapy recording was no match for fate." Hillary's face clouds, "But what if I don't want to go! What if I want to stay? It may have been hard, but I know I can do things differently." Upon seeing Heidi, Hillary stops and composes herself, "Oh, I'm so sorry. First, Steve. Now me. Come here, Heidi." Hillary picks her niece up and cradles her, cherishing the feeling of her cheek on Heidi's.

The little girl's body shakes with sobs. "This can't be real," she says into Hillary's shoulder.

As Hillary lets Heidi down, Molly kneels and gives her daughter a kiss. "You know I love you very much, don't you?"

Heidi nods and gives her mother another squeeze, then turns to Hillary sniffling, "Aunt Hillary, letting Daddy go was the hardest thing I ever did in my life. I don't know how I'm going to live without you." Then, with a deep breath, Heidi continues, "But, at least I get to say goodbye." With another sniff, the little girl looks deeply into her aunt's eyes, "Goodbye, Auntie." She gives Hillary another hug and feels Moa's hand on her shoulder.

Moa, now glows with a bright yellow energy. She is so blindingly bright, Heidi puts her hand up to shield her eyes.

With a hand still on Heidi's shoulder, Moa sends that bright light from her heart into first Heidi's then Molly's heart. The mother and daughter soon radiate light as brightly as Moa.

"Remember how I appeared to you all in Hawaii?" Moa continues to send her healing love to them. "Well, Hillary will learn to do the same thing. It may take a while, but we'll get there."

"How long is a while?" Heidi marvels at her own iridescent hand, then Molly's, then back at Moa.

"I'll tell you what." Moa hands Heidi a silver coin with three parallel wavy lines on it.

"Ku's family coin!" Heidi says excitedly.

"Actually," Moa says with a twinkle in her eye. "It is a healer coin. Only those with healing qualities may keep it in their possession. When you feel this vibrate, you'll know we're about to visit."

"I love you, Mol. Love you, Heidi." Hillary calls.

"I'll never forget you, Auntie Hillary." The last thing Heidi sees as Hillary and Moa disappear are Hillary's hands waving goodbye through the mist.

Heidi and Molly shimmer into nothingness and then reanimate at sunset on the sand near their home at Waikiki Beach in Hawaii.

The warm breeze tousles Heidi's long brown hair and plays at Molly's t-shirt. The gorgeous, fiery sun sends rays into the water, which sparkles with amber and gold.

"I still don't know how long 'a while' is to Moa," Heidi says, looking up at her mom with a smile and holding out the silver coin—the orange sun playing off the wavy stamped lines, "but I'm going to carry this coin with me always."

Epilogue

A beautiful woman walks along Waikiki Beach at sunset while supporting the arm of an elderly white-haired gentleman who struggles with each step in the sand. Tendrils of her long, dark-brown hair flutter around her neck.

"It's okay, Mr. Baker. "I know it's tough getting around these days. My grandmother has the same problems."

"Thanks, Heidi," The man continues on despite his challenge. "Getting old sucks."

As they reach the end of the parking lot and begin to dust the sand off of their feet, Heidi's pocket begins to vibrate. Her heart flutters as she pulls out a silver coin and rubs her thumb over the indentations of three wavy lines, tracing the smooth metal as she has done for so many years, tracing and waiting, tracing and hoping.

The coin continues to vibrate and, looking out to the misty swirls rolling in from the sea, Heidi holds the treasure up to her heart and begins to weep.

About the Author

Tricia Stewart Shiu is an award-winning, screenwriter, author and playwright, but her passion lies in creating mystical stories. Her latest series, The Moa Books, which includes Moa, The Statue of Ku and The Iron Shinto, were, by far her favorite to write.

Learn More about Moa
Facebook:
http://www.facebook.com/MoaBook
Website:
http://www.Moa-Book.com
Moa Blog:
http://tstewartshiu.wordpress.com
Follow Tricia Stewart Shiu on Twitter:
@tstewartshiu

www.ingramcontent.com/pod-product-compliance
Lightning Source LLC
Chambersburg PA
CBHW072103170626
46813CB00004B/1434